# Carousel

T E Williams

IreeSky Fiction, LLC© ISBN: 9798654356222 KDP 6/2020
Trisha E Williams/IreeSky

## Chapter #1 – "The Spot"

Shardae Richardson stood at the old fashioned, rusted, white stove burning visible hairs off the defrosted chicken wings she was preparing for her grandmother. The wings had been left sitting in cool, clean water in the sink. She painstakingly rubbed each wing plucking the remaining feathers shifting between the lit eye burner of the stove and the sink. She held the wing over the eye burner and the licks of the blue flame would sizzle as the hairs vanished. Shardae carefully inspected to see if there were any hairs tucked away pulling the skin with her fingers.

After the last wing was clean, she placed them flat on several streaming paper towels. She seasoned them well, flipped them around in hot sauce, and checked the heat on the oil waiting to receive them. "Perfect!" She said wiping her hands on her apron. Frying chicken wings was something Shardae did every Friday night. This was no family meal she was preparing. The Richardsons owned the hottest most popular undercover crap house in Trenton. Hattie Richardson, Shardae's grandmother was considered the respected diva of the crap house where folks came in droves after the bars closed to press their luck at the card game, dice, or darts. High stakes were garnered at Hattie's, and on a good night, you could walk out with a thousand dollars and a chicken wing platter.

Hattie had five strong sons who knew their positions in the large connected backyard sheds to protect Hattie's investment. Hattie herself was a big woman who carried, so all knew not to try Ms. Hattie. She didn't have to pull it out often, but the rumor was that she kept a .22 in her bosom. Her face looked innocent enough, and most who don't known Hattie would mistake her for an old church woman. Hattie Richardson ran her establishment with an iron fist, and her cash-savvy children watched every dollar, every strange face, every hand played.

The large backyard sheds were deceptive to the untrained eyes of the police, because they looked like simple man-cave style sheds for lawnmowers and snow shovels. They were only accessible from the alley, and customers had to know the special knock or password to enter. Hattie's eldest, Jake, changed it every weekend, and not just anybody could show up at Hattie's. Shardae's five uncles were street-smart mathematicians. Hattie birthed one drug rehabilitated daughter, Karen, Shardae's birth mother who worked the crap house. A special section of one of the sheds was cordoned off for Hattie's office where Jake would safely count the money and monitor the doors through video surveillance. Hattie would greet the guests early but would retire leaving everything to her diligent sons at midnight. Last orders for food had to be in by that time, and Shardae and her friend Capri would serve the food and collect the money.

Shardae was just as sharp as Hattie when it came to a dollar, and she kept her weapon in the small of her back exposed over the apron strings. She knew she didn't have to worry with her uncles there. Jake watched everything Capri did only trusting family hands. She would never cross that line having so much love for Shardae and Ms. Hattie. Shardae's other uncles, Mike,

Paul, Nathan, and the youngest, Tyrell appreciated that Capri worked hard for them and kept family secrets. She requested the night off.

Shardae dropped the wings into flour and into the hot oil. She washed her hands of flour and hot sauce, changed into a new apron, and walked out the back door of the house down the path to the main shed with a platter of wings. Second in command, Mike, opened the door for her after seeing her through the sliding window. His post was the door of the main shed. "Hey Mike, last batch is dropped, and so will I right after that!" She said to her silent uncle, the exact opposite of Jake, who was extremely vocal. He just nodded snatching a wing off the tray licking his fingers. Hattie sold a combo plate of 8 wings w/fries for $15 dollars, and most would offer Shardae the whole $20 bill. Shardae occasionally put 9 wings on each plate anyway. She collected the cash and made her way back to the kitchen.

When the last wings were drained of grease, she brought the tray of wing platters out noticing an odd car slowly approaching in the alley. Uncle Mike heard the unusual pace of her steps and snatched open the window. "What's up?!!" He whispered. "SHUT DOWN!" She mustered barely

moving her lips. She rushed the wing tray back into the house, but there were 40 S.W.A.T members in and around the house, weapons drawn. She dropped the tray and assumed the position.

Hattie Richardson was booked along with her granddaughter, her sons, and some of the patrons of the crap house, a $4,200 loss for the night.

## Chapter #2 – "Round 'N Round"

When the court date arrived for Hattie Richardson, her family had already been released or bailed out and most of the customers were free pending court dates. Hattie was held having had prior charges for repeat offenses. There was no bail. Shardae, who's 17, was released to mother, Karen, who had just been released from the county jail herself after a 3-year stint for credit card theft. All her life, Karen was in and out of jail for various scams, and Shardae was able to live with Hattie, who had also served time in jail for like crimes. They had been on Social Services receiving welfare assistance for as long as they had been alive.

"Next case please!" The judge demanded as the docket number was read by the court clerk. Hattie's public defender stood with her as she was told to rise in the orange, large-fitting, distasteful jumper with D O C written on the front under the V-neck. The female prosecutor stood with folded arms at the sight of Hattie Richardson. The judge asked, "Whoa! Hattie Richardson? Not again!" Hattie and the attorney swayed. The indictment was handed to the judge who kept her index finger over her mouth reading it. Hattie's attorney began to speak, but the judge cut him off, "You are charged with running an unlawful business in the County of Mercer, running a continuous public nuisance in the County of Mercer, and a laundry list of other charges you've been before me for the past 20 years! They shut you down at one place and you just open up at a new location!"

The judge looked into Hattie's eyes holding the indictment high. She poked her lips to the left. "Is this how you want to spend your senior years? Aren't you tired of standing before me? I know I'm tired of it!" He asked with animated motion clutching the paper to his own chest. He shook his head when he didn't receive an answer. "Ms. Richardson, what is so glamourous about this continuous illegal activity you're accused of in my County???" The public defender tried to intervene holding up his pointed finger, "Uh…Your Honor, with respect…" The judge swung the paper back and forth as if to say, 'Ah, Ah, Ah, I know you're representing her, but I'm not *really* expecting an answer.' Hattie knew better anyway. She would never say anything to incriminate herself. She also knew some things that the judge and prosecutor did not know.

"Ugh! How do you plead?" He asked.

Hattie's attorney asked for a moment with his client which was granted. After whispers and nods, the attorney then asked to approach the bench. Both the female prosecutor and the lawycr walkcd up to thc judge and returned to their prospective tables. The prosecutor side-eyed Hattie with her jaws tight thumbing through papers. The bailiff handed her a copy of what the judge had in front of him.

The judge informed, "Ms. Richardson, I've just learned your public defender highlighted a significant technicality in the hasty search warrant issued by Judge Ryland on the night of the raid of your home on Lamberton Street. I understand the warrant specified the main home dwelling...? Well, apparently, he presented this signed lease as well, by the occupant of a separate dwelling structure on your property labeled Apartments A, B, and C, as rental properties. Who is Jake Mitchell ma'am?"

Hattie Richardson stood still now, "My tenant." The public defender had submitted Jake's signed lease as evidence of paid residency of a separate dwelling. The rental income was reported monthly to Social Services just low enough not to sanction Hattie's welfare check. This meant Hattie's actual residence was the only structure noted on the warrant which was to be searched. When they raided her three 'sheds', they violated the issued warrant's intended terminology. Hattie knew the system and all the property owner's rights according to the Agency's policy.

Welfare was aware she was a homeowner with vacant apartments, but Jake's lease was so recently dated that rental income didn't have to be reported until the following month. Hattie was smart. Not one physical contraband evidence was found in her home, so she knew she was off the hook for all charges and for fraud. The corners of her mouth turned up into a slight grin. She knew she got over when she watched the judge carefully inspect the warrant which did not include the sheds or Jake's name.

When the gavel hit, Hattie was free. Shardae and her uncles were relieved. They all walked with her out of the courtroom and only Shardae looked back at the judge who was shaking his head. The prosecutor slammed her files down on the table in anger. "Case dismissed." The frustrated judge said quietly.

The judge looked back at Shardae retreating. This wasn't Shardae's first time in court. She saw her mother Karen's many court proceedings in her young life. She heard Hattie's name called by judges to stand many, many times too. Shardae knew the historical story of her grandmother's mother who had died in prison for scamming a naïve man who wanted to remain in the United States to become a citizen out of $100,000. The man set out to use her, but Essie Richardson knew how to use the system to her advantage. The poor foreigner had no idea who the Richardsons were!

Everything Essie did to make a dollar, she taught Hattie, and of course, Hattie taught her sons and her only daughter Karen, who was a seasoned prime example for Shardae. At just 10 years of age, Shardae had a very unique skill. She could remember figures and the order they were in. When she was much younger, Karen noticed that the child could identify cars by their license plates. She could tell whether a car had already passed them as they walked. She differentiated between the colors of the state which distributed the plate, the sequence of letters, numbers, characters, spaces, etc. Shardae could even describe who drove it.

Over the years, Karen developed Shardae's talent by writing numbers down on index cards. By the time she was 14, she could glance at large groupings of numbers and repeat them perfectly. This would be valuable later, and Karen knew it. Her uncles and grandmother were impressed by Shardae's memory of figures. She'd be useful to the family in this way.

The first time Karen was released from serving time, she worked at the local Seven Eleven. The clerks were responsible for issuing money orders to customers. This was before technological advances made it difficult to scam due to watermarks and 3D layering which weren't available in the 90's. Karen developed the perfect scam by making duplicates of the money orders purchased by the customers. When she felt they were catching on, she'd work at another outlet which distributed money orders. She used different names, ID's, and Social Security numbers of her theft victims. She used this information to get hired for various places of employment. The victims were mostly people who had been careless with their identification. Karen looked for easy targets like folks who left purses in the shopping cart or in the glove compartment.

Karen would have entire yard sales in front of Hattie's house selling whatever she stole. She sold socks, clothes, cleaning products, shoes, hair bows, artwork; whatever was in demand in the 'hood. When Hattie was younger, she sold tobacco, meat, eggs, road maps, pots and pans, Avon, Mary Kay, Tupperware, Amway, Popular Club, life insurance policies, burial plots, and anything else short of human organs. Great-grandmother Essie was rumored to have read palms, futures, run matchmaking scams, sell doctored train tickets, and sell moonshine, right out of her own back shed. They always had a gambling establishment running on the weekends.

Essie, Hattie, Karen, and Shardae always sold dinners right out of the house for folks who didn't feel like cooking. The neighborhood knew they could count on the Richardson household for a good, quick meal. Shardae had been in the kitchen since she was knee high. She could cook anything from scratch at 10 years old and most people thought it was Ms. Hattie's cooking. She made homemade cornbread, cakes, pies, greens, macaroni and cheese, and of course, fried fish and chicken wings especially well.

Jake and her other uncles broke into the numbers game early as teens, so they always knew the old number runners who taught them everything they needed to know to hustle. Essie's 1st husband taught them weaponry and Hattie's husband taught them to fight. Their younger brother, Tyrell, was the first to try his hand at selling weed and was successful at it for years until he earned his first charge. He began to hustle T-Shirts and scented oils to earn cash. He wasn't much older than Shardae. Their father died before he was born. He wasn't built for hard time and Hattie was happy with the slap on the wrist the judge gave him explaining that he had been following an older group of boys.

Paul and Nate were twins, in and out on various simple nuisance charges, but Mike and Jake had done 8 years between the two of them. If you were to print their criminal records, you could wallpaper Hattie's house.

At the time of the raid, all Hattie's kids were home. The systemic oppression of the 'hood made it difficult to find work once you had criminal charges, so Hattie had her children work for her. Her children's names were known by the entire police force, and Trenton is so small. It didn't matter what ward Hattie moved to, her sons were infamous in town.

When Karen went away to County last time, everyone tried to come together to keep the crap house popular. They all had their hands in other illegitimate ventures but were smart to run their entities carefully.

Shardae knew what they all were into and where they could be found. Jake had systems in place to counter anything coming. This is why they had a select group of repeat customers in the crap house. Mike had warned Jake of the increase crowds on Friday nights, but Jake thought he had it handled. He listened to only Hattie whose hand would itch if there was good money present. She could be seen scratching her hand and Jake knew by that sign if it was going to be a prosperous night.

Mike Richardson was quiet, but dangerous. Jake was a fast talker who could pretty much BS his way out of trouble. Mike was a 'take no prisoners' type of brother who, when backed into a corner, would have no problem shooting his way out. He had mastered the art of observation. The night of the raid, Mike got some of the cash and all the guns into the hidden compartment in the wall before they kicked in the door. He sat on the stool by the door with a toothpick in his teeth and his hands raised. Jake was talking non-stop the entire course of the raid! "What y'all got??? Nothing! We're playing cards right here with our friends, shooting pool, having drinks! Y'all ain't got nothing!" He could still be heard while getting ushered into the wagon.

Shardae knew the routine. She placed her hands behind her own back not offering any words, but she and Hattie needed few words to have a conversation. Hattie just winked at her and said, "You already know." Shardae just answered, "Yup." She had been witnessing this routine all her life, and she knew she wasn't going to be locked up long. Deep down, she knew none of Hattie's charges would stick. Hattie made the front page of the local paper 11 times.

What they all were wondering was who snitched for the raid to be set up by S.W.A.T. in the first place? Jake's money was on Capri. He didn't believe all this just happened on her night off. He was already running his mouth about it before he was released. When they were freed, he made his feelings clear with Shardae who challenged him, but it seemed his mind was made up. She told him that anyone could have been released by offering them up like a chicken wing platter.

## *Chapter #3 – "Making Moves"*

Before Hattie's sons brought her home, they began repairing the kicked in door and chaos left by the raid to the sheds. Shardae took inventory of the walk-in freezer to see what was salvageable; 12 cases of chicken wings, 2 cases of whiting, 7 bags of French fries, and 10 cases of breaded shrimp. She reported it to Hattie, who sat in her office evaluating her mortgage papers.

Because of Karen's constant incarcerations, Shardae had become comfortable calling Hattie 'Ma' throughout her lifetime. All of Hattie's children called her Hattie, including Karen. When Shardae said, 'Ma', everyone knew she was talking to Hattie. She called her mother

Karen. Hattie's children called Essie 'Big Ma' when she was alive.

Shardae saw Hattie Richardson flipping the pages over as if she was seeking a specific document. She hadn't notice Shardae standing in the doorway. "Ma?" She said finally getting Hattie's attention. "I missed two days of school so I'm going tomorrow, okay?" Hattie looked up at her, "Shar, it looks like I'll need you this summer, when I get this figured out. Go'on and finish out the year, you're gonna have to work this summer, legit." Shardae knew exactly what Hattie meant, on the books. She handed Hattie the slip with the written inventory as Mike entered. "'Sup, Unc?" She said in passing. "Hey baby girl. Are you going back to school?" He asked. "Yeah, I was just telling Ma, tomorrow." She answered. Mike knew this was her last year of school. No one in the family had finished high school due to their lifestyle, from Essie on down. Shardae was upheld as the light.

Hattie said, "Mike, round everybody up." He left quietly to get everyone together in the office to hear Hattie's announcement. "Shardae, sweep up that glass on the other side." She ordered. Shardae grabbed the push broom and began sweeping the main hall between the attached sheds. She could still hear their voices and listened intently. Hattie began to reveal her plan to relocate by selling the property. "Listen, my name has come up on the waiting list for City Side and Trenton Housing Authority at the same time. I'm going to take advantage of it. Jake, you'll be maintaining the place they give me at City Side. Mike, you got Roger Gardens. Me and Shardae are staying in South Trenton to keep our customers, but I need another house in the cut where we can setup shop. Nate, you start looking somewhere we can be free from nonsense." All three gentlemen gave Hattie nods.

"Paul, you're going to have to put in some leg work to let folks know where we are. Jake and Tyrell, you scout out who could've ratted us out. Young people talk. Karen, we need some quick cash to recover what we lost. I hope you already got something started." Karen rubbed her palms together, "Yes ma'am, I'm working customers at ShopRite on #33, West Trenton at Marrazzo's, and got three Go Fund Me accounts for Jason's cancer." Nate asked, "Who the hell is Jason?" Karen shook her head laughing, "Who the hell knows! It's up to $998 though!" They all laughed. Hattie waved with the back of her hand and they all dispersed.

Shardae ran across to the other side of the shed she was sweeping so they wouldn't catch her eavesdropping. Hattie came out of the office to where Shardae was sweeping. "Shar I need you to get dressed and come with me." There were these times when having Shardae with her garnered sympathy from onlookers. Just before the raid, she had Shardae check the status of her own FAFSA for post high school funding and two other accounts which they applied for in different names; they were pending.

Shardae placed the broom in the corner after sweeping the shards of glass into the dustpan. She went to get dressed as Hattie requested. Hattie got a message that her bank accounts were no longer frozen. She and Shardae headed out of the door to the bank.

Hattie had Shardae apply for a student loan in her own name, small business loans at two other banks using Karen's fake ID cards, and doctored paperwork on the property which was raided, and Hattie herself applied for emergency assistance with the City and County Welfare offices. She was instantly approved for $400 in emergency food stamps but a grant for cash assistance was pending to see if she was in good standing. The City approved a grant for $1,500 for first month's rent and security for a new lease she created with fake names. Vouchers were dispersed on the spot paid directly to the *landlord*, which, in reality was Hattie Richardson, for the raided Lamberton house, and for *Apartment A*, a lease in Shardae's name.

By the afternoon, Hattie and Shardae had applied and had been approved for over $3,200 in assistance through the fake identifications Karen provided. Two days later, Shardae received her acceptance into Mercer County Community College pending graduation. Her major was Culinary Studies.

All Hattie's sons had done their homework and reported in. Both Paul and Nate informed them that Trenton gambling was dry since the raid. "Everybody wants to know when we back up, Hattie." He said. Jake paced the floor, "We good! I got us a spot over on Centre. It has a shed way in the back of the house like here, and the alley is full of brush leading directly to it. It has two doors to the shed, just need to get it cleaned up. It's got like tires and debris back there." He said. Hattie said, "That's good, get her done. Y'all change two things, daily draws & daily withdrawals! Jake, anybody hit the street number?" Hattie asked. "We had two, but nothing major." Jake told her. "Tyrell, what'd you find out?" She asked curious about the snitch.

Tyrell could get factual information in the streets quickly like a confidential informant. Everybody knew who his people were and would tell him the truth. He had such a way with people, a true salesman. He answered, "Hattie, I'm still trying to find out. This sting must've been something that they weren't investigating long, because somebody would have told me. This wasn't on the radar. Jake would've smelled it. I'm gonna find out though." Jake stopped pacing. "Nah, I ain't slippin'. This was some inside stuff, Hattie. Call Shardae in here!" He demanded. When she came in, he asked, "Where's Capri?" Shardae knew what they had all been standing around discussing. Her heart sunk. She didn't want her friend to be under the microscope. "Unc she had death in the family, she don't even know we were raided!" Shardae said defending Capri. Mike spoke up. "Maaaaaan, that girl like family. What she got to gain? Jake, this is not the first time I heard you ask about that girl, she ain't got *snitch* in her."

Hattie quelled all the noise with her deep voice. "Listen, we're not going to point fingers at Capri until we find out more information. Jake, you know I don't have trust for a lot of people, but Capri comes in here, does her job, and comes back every Friday. The girl never so much as took more than her nightly tips. Let's not jump to conclusions, but Shardae, you keep an eye on that girl. If she got picked up for something, you need to find out if she got any charges, a reason to rat us out, understand?" Hattie ordered. "Yes ma'am. I mean we're close, but I watch Capri like y'all do. Plus, she's got pictures of herself in Greensboro at the funeral, and everything's sad and solemn on her FB posts with her dad. Her mom left them! It ain't Capri, Ma."

Jake shot back, "You don't know if those are staged pictures or what, so just don't get comfortable with seeing what you see on Facebook. I trust nobody but family, baby girl." Mike silently sat with his arms folded, then changed the subject directed toward Jake, "Whassup with that City Side?" He asked Jake. "Karen, you gotta get ID's with better credit because they done started credit checks." Jake answered looking at Karen ignoring Mike. Karen was pretty sure those ID's she stole were from folks with common, ambiguous names, so that an authority couldn't tell the ethnicity or nationality. They were age appropriate for Hattie, herself, or Shardae, and she had even lifted ID's with faces which favored her brothers. She had it down to a science. "You can't tell a credit score by an ID, but if they look like they good, I gotchu." Karen said.

Hattie listened and continued. "Good. Roger Gardens got me on Eisenhower, so y'all get a U-Haul from off Brunswick only, don't try Budget, too many new faces. Let's get moving. House items to Centre with the spot's stuff to the shed. Work quickly at nightfall. Paul and Nate, y'all furnish Eisenhower from HomeFront donations and Goodwill. Tyrell, keep your ear to the ground. Karen, I need the White girl, for my next move. Make sure she's just plain looking this time and get her some *Manager* work ID's for Amazon. Cecil still manages, right? Nate, I need a temporary storage from Haji the Arab. Karen...here." She handed Karen a Trac Phone and a Capital One card in the name of Judith Pigliano. "I need her to apply for a cash advance, then Karen, take her to Amazon. Nate, you build the wall safe in the new shed for the cash and one in the floor for my guns. Shardae, get ready for school tomorrow. Jake, let's count."

Hattie dismissed everyone. She and Jake counted the cash they had accumulated. Afterward, Hattie and Jake shopped to replenish the liquor for the crap house. Hattie's crap house was open by the next Friday on Centre

Street with their same old customers. Capri had returned to help Shardae with the food orders.

The White girl Hattie referred to, Monica Frein, set up an investment account in the name of Judith Pigliano with Charles Schwab for an initial $1,500. She would actively maintain this account as Judith Pigliano for a fee, which she understood. Monica had made investments for Hattie in fictitious names for years and could be trusted. The key was to use Monica's face and skill in investing which benefited them both. Monica used to make investments for Essie when Hattie was young. They had several cloaked real estate companies in New Jersey which were bought and sold quickly for profit. Monica wasn't used often, but in hard times such as these. Karen now dealt with her directly, and Hattie bowed out gracefully earning great dividends in the early 2000's.

Cecil Clark was family, a nephew of Hattie's who managed Amazon Fulfillment in Hamilton. Occasionally he'd provide ID's on the low as if the person was an employee.

Hattie could no longer pay employees of the Motor Vehicle Commission due to Homeland Security's stance on identity theft which came with hefty federal charges. She had gotten away with so much before these penalties were installed, but always found a way around it until recently. Those days were over. With Cecil in this power position, she could maintain.

Karen would open new accounts at Macy's and JC Penney through kids who were due to graduate high school, and she'd maintain those active accounts. She'd buy bedding and clothing items and return them for cash or sell the items for a higher cost right out the trunk of her car. The cycle would repeat in intervals of two, on at least eight students at a time, then she'd shred the cards.

Nate and Paul bid on foreclosed houses repairing them for rental profit legitimately as a front for Hattie. They worked daily refurbishing and flipping houses to rent. There was no way to obtain evidence that what they were doing was illegal. Even when authorities dug deep, there was nothing they could pin on them which would stick. Countless times, Karen would shop spending between $700-$900 using fictitious student credit cards then report the card stolen immediately afterward avoiding surveillance cameras.

Hattie also used little known sneaky ways to infiltrate utility assistance programs, lunch programs, tax programs, even the cable company. She'd simply send Jake up the pole for cable television. Jake knew how to restore public service electricity to her home if she ever got cut off. If they found out, he'd just use the neighbor's outdoor socket to light Hattie's house. They'd never know.

Hattie Richardson was a professional scam artist who taught her children what she was taught; how to take advantage of the systems in place intended to help the low-income poverty-stricken masses. It had been a lifestyle for generations.

# Chapter #4 – "Shardae's Graduation"

On June 13th, Shardae received her cap & gown and her senior photos. Her family was very happy for her. Karen threw her a party in the Centre Street back yard shed. She invited Capri and her friends from the hospitality course who had been an encouragement. Shardae, Tyrell and Capri decorated with glittery banners and stars for the party. She would not have to prepare chicken wings this night. She was the star of the family. Mike Richardson cooked the food with Capri's help.

On the party menu was, hot wings, potato salad, (the good ole' tangy, relishy kind), collard greens with smoked turkey, browned macaroni and cheese, jumbo fried shrimp, well-seasoned crabs, (#1 male), and buttered rolls. Hattie hired a deejay for the event and gave her a beautiful set of stainless-steel cooking utensils that were Essie Richardson's. Hattie let her hair down donning a pair of jeans, which Hattie Richardson never wore. She only wore dresses. Capri set her hair in a young folk's style and polished Hattie's nails, made her face up to a youthful glow, and helped her pick out some Air Max's so she could feel fly.

Capri sat on the counter swinging her legs as Mike cooked the last batch of the crabs. They caught a glimpse at each other over the steaming pot when Mike stood between her dangling legs to kiss her. When they pulled back from one another, Jake walked into the kitchen, saw their interaction, and backed slowly out. No one knew they were enamored with one another; they were careful. Mike was 10 years older than Capri who was 19. Shardae knew Capri liked her uncle, but never realized their feelings were mutual.

Jake felt he had more ammunition to launch his campaign against Capri. This relationship was not something Jake expected at all. He figured he'd bide his time and wait for an opportunity.

In the interim, as difficult as it was for Jake to do, he kept silent, not a 'Jake' characteristic. This was juicy, this would give him leverage in his decision making with Hattie. Mike assumed Jake was Hattie's right hand, being the eldest, but he had no idea *he* was actually Hattie's favorite.

Hattie sat in her office with a woman who sought to have her future told concerning her husband's health. Hattie flipped through tarot cards and placed three cards down in front of her, good health, good fortune, and a two-faced woman, the Hierophant. Hattie who deemed herself a priestess knew what it meant. The woman's husband would not live, but afterward, she would be healthier in mind and prosperity from his death. The two faces represented a major turning point in her life. Hattie knew the woman would not accept the reading, so she worded it so that the woman would favor her counsel.

She smiled and tilted her head, "You have drawn the card of good health. I wouldn't worry, *you'll* be alright. That'll be $100 dear." Hattie held out her hand and the woman stood. "Oh! Thank you! Ms. Hattie you always know what you're talking about! That's why I only deal with you!" She said digging in her purse.

Hattie snatched the bills and slid them into her bra ushering the woman out. She handed her a sachet of black tea leaves and a black talisman to wear on her neck. "Drink this twice a day and rub this charm in the morning only."

Shardae entered the office as she left. "Ma, she drew Prudence? I remember what you told me about Prudence. Hope you told her it has two meanings!" Hattie threw her head back, "I had to give her good news, we're going to need her soon! What do you need, child?" Hattie asked. "Ma I was thinking about that financial aid thing we filled out. I think I want to go for real. You know? To Mercer for Culinary."

Hattie looked at her granddaughter seriously. "Look baby girl, I got use for that when it's approved. It's bad enough they 'bout to cut my stamps because you'll be 18, I just need to stack a l'il bit before they cut me off for good. Besides, I need you around here for some things I have coming up. It's a good thing, you graduating from high school and all. We're all proud of you. Not one of my children has their high school diploma. You got to slow down a l'il bit though. Maybe next year. We just got back up from the raid, we got to recover, baby."

Hattie dissuaded her from thinking about higher education. She knew her grandmother needed her and knew Karen would be happy with her if she stayed home to help her. She knew Hattie would not be eligible for food stamps without her, therefore, would not be able to supply food for the crap house. "Oh, I was just reading the school brochure. It would be like an 18-month program. It doesn't even cost that much." Hattie shuffled pass her, "Tyrell!" She hollered. He came in asking her bidding. "Take Shardae to the shed so she can enjoy her party, please, she talkin' crazy." Tyrell started walking behind Shardae to get her moving. "Shardae, before you leave, turn over the three top cards, and I'll tell you if there's any cooking to be done in your future." Shardae took the Prudence card and used it to swipe three new cards over walking out without looking at them. She was disappointed in Hattie's reply about school. She and Tyrell went to the party where the mood suddenly heightened.

When Hattie saw the reveal, she kicked off her sneakers. She looked in their direction walking out then down at the cards again. Unbeknownst to Shardae, she drew the Ten of Pentacles (success, fame, and long-term stability), the Strength card, (mastering the ability to hone emotions and anxieties), and the Hanged Man (gaining a new perspective).

Hattie mumbled, "You just might be the sweetest card ever dealt." She shook her right hand over the deck. "Mm, Mm, Mm", she mumbled shaking her head. She put her shoes back on and headed back to the shed to party with the young people.

Jake walked up to her with an envelope to present to Shardae. She quieted the music and noise by holding up one hand calling her to the forefront. "Shardae, this is for you." She said handing her the envelope. Tyrell rushed over with a bouquet of roses. People were holding up their cell phones recording the emotional scene for social media. "Congratulations baby!" She said with tears embracing Shardae. Capri yelled, "Open it! Open it girl!" as they applauded. Shardae opened the envelope pulling out five $100 bills and a beautiful crystal necklace. Capri joined the hug and the tears began to fall. "I'm so proud of you." Capri said. She had left school to get her GED in the middle of the school year 2017.

Paul and Nathan came over sticking wads of money in Shardae's hand and Hattie signaled the deejay to spin. They partied until the wee hours of the morning and celebrated Shardae's accomplishment. Folks asked Shardae what she was going to do now that high school was over. Her answer was simple and short. "I'm going to help out Ma." Hattie smiled harder each time the answer was expressed.

Capri and Mike dipped off into the night to a clandestine hideout beyond the alley exiting at different times. The 1 o'clock regulars had come to play cards, and Shardae's crew went into the house. Later, after her crowd dispersed, Shardae entered Hattie's office alone to see what she had drawn. A big smile appeared on her face. She then closed her eyes turning over one last card from the top of the deck for confirmation. It was Death and Resurrection, (an end and new beginning).

## *Chapter #5 – "Dividends"*

Shardae awoke to a hot summer July day thinking about school. She picked up the brochure and began scanning the page with the Culinary Studies course which she earmarked by folding the corner. Karen tapped on her bedroom door and she stashed it on the side of her bed. "Come in." She said. "Heyyy Karen, what's up?" Karen sat at the foot of her bed. Shardae asked, "What's wrong?" Karen hesitated, but eventually managed to speak, "Shardae my hand's been itching all morning! Let me use your phone to call Monica Frein."

Shardae rolled over tossing Karen her cell phone. Karen vigorously depressed the numbers. Monica picked up on the 3rd ring. "Hello?" She answered. "Hey girl, you got something for me?" Karen asked hopeful. Monica had been working on Hattie's phony portfolio for about two months and investors were pouring into the account set up by Monica. "Yeah! Pull out?" She asked. "Yeah, my hand itching like crazy! What are we looking at?" She asked Monica who put her on hold. When she clicked in again, she said, "We got about $6k, I'd leave it in there!" Karen was excited. "Nah! I need that right quick, cash out! Meet me at the check cashing place with your Amazon ID, and don't be all flashy, just be plain." Monica agreed and hung up.

Monica immediately called each investor with her professional phone voice explaining that their stock option which she suggested didn't do too well. It suddenly nosedived and they were in the red. She advised them to cut their losses. Each time, the investor expressed anger disappointed in her tip and asked to speak to her manager. Karen would disguise her voice pretending to fire herself on the spot. She never used the same investors twice and kept everything separate from her true clients which earned excellent dividends from her work. Her portfolio was filled with savvy investors. She took advantage of the ones who were new to investing or were less knowledgeable using them for Hattie's dummy account. She funneled funds in and out making money for the Richardson family and a nice nest egg for herself.

Monica Frein could sit next to you at a Starbucks in disguise and you would never know she was smart. Hattie counted on that, as did Essie. She could look old or young, she could be a stripper or an accountant, and what Hattie loved was that she wasn't greedy. When she put on her Wall Street attire carrying her leather briefcase, she could charm anyone into opening a prison cell or the judge's chambers if need be. Hattie paid her up front and paid her well. She just needed Karen's ID's.

She drove to the usual Trenton check cashing spots presenting four different Amazon Manager's ID's, one with Judith Pigliano. The laundered checks totaling over $6,000 were verified by the clerks who called to clear them by Cecil. Monica made sure they weren't over 30 days old. At the last spot, she stuffed the cash into her back jean pocket and threw her hoodie over her scraggly ponytail. Monica opened the passenger seat of Karen's car handing her the money for Hattie. "Let me know when to start up again." She said. "Oh, it'll be a while Monica. We're back on track now." Karen said counting the money. Monica exited the parking lot.

When Karen entered the house, Hattie asked. "How'd it go?" Karen told her all went 'smooth as silk' handing her the cash. "Cashed out at six Hattie. White girl said call if you need her again. "Six huh? That's good for a month. You told her I could only use her once or twice a year, right?" Hattie asked licking her thumb to count the cash. "She knows." Hattie peeled off $1,000 and gave it to Karen stuffing the rest into her bra. "Listen, call Shardae in here, will you?" She demanded. Karen called Shardae right from where she stood. She was curious to know what Hattie wanted. When Shardae came to her, she stood watching Hattie count. "Shar, you hear back from the financial aid people?" Hattie asked. "Ma, you mean me, personally? Or Jane and John Doe?"

"Don't be a smart butt girl, you know what I mean!" Hattie shot back. "Go check the emails to see if they contacted you child!" Shardae looked at the several emails in her phone and saw three separate messages of congratulations from Mercer County Community College. There were items she needed to prove on a To Do list to receive checks for school, and she learned she received a scholarship for $1,000 to further her education which she hadn't expected. Her Hospitality teacher had applied on her behalf.

Shardae said, "Ma, they want us to present more information for the applicants. This ain't gone work!" Hattie continued to count her money. "Yes, it will, baby I've been doing this a long time. I just need to go up there and…" Shardae cut her off. "No Ma, they do everything electronically now. The jig is up!" Hattie looked up from counting. Karen's eyes darted back and forth between them. "Not everybody uses computers Shar. Believe me, I'll get it done. What'd they say about yours?" Hattie questioned. "Yeah, I'm eligible, but it's got the Lamberton Street address on it, remember?" Shardae said. "It's not going to matter Shar, because I have a lease in your name with dependents in the household. Don't worry about nothing, I got this." Hattie said. She peeled of two $100 dollar bills and handed them to Shardae. "Thank you, Ma." She said but didn't walk away. "Yes?" Hattie asked her regarding her hesitation.

"Nevermind…well, I'm just saying, Ma, um…I may as well go'on and go to classes then." She said looking at the floor. Karen chose this moment to casually walk out. "You know what Shardae? Go'on and go! You wanted to all along! Go'on! You know I need you around here!" Hattie hollered raising her voice. "You get well taken care of 'round here, never wanted for nothing! I don't understand you, child! You come and go as you please, don't contribute nothing to this family, and spoiled! You've gotten used to living comfortable!"

Shardae wanted to say something, but she had a point. She didn't ask much of her, not really. Then she suddenly found herself arguing with Hattie and had never intended to. "Ma, I always do what you want to do, we *all* do, but this is something I want to do for me, understand? I can't stay around here and wait on your needs hand and foot like *she* do!" She said throwing her head toward Karen. "I got to experience things for myself! I want to go to school; want to get my degree in cooking! I'm good at it, Ma, and you know it!"

Hattie was now standing, and that is never a good sign. Shardae was going off on a tangent, saying things she would never say, things she couldn't take back. "Ma, I don't have no social life! I can't even join Capri when she do stuff because I'm always here! I see my best friend on Friday night when we're working the crap house and that's it! No mall, no movies, no double dates, no nothing! I want to go to school! I want to do something different than *your* plan for my life! All we do is scam! Scam, scam, SCAM, every day just to live! If it wasn't for me, you wouldn't be getting no check! All we do is scam people! This ain't no life!"

Hattie drew back her hand and slapped the taste out of Shardae's mouth. Tears formed, Shardae felt heat coming from out of her neck which shot down to her heart, then up to her cheek. She had never been hit in her face by her grandmother. It took her breath away. Shardae launched the $200 on the floor and left her presence.

She ran upstairs, packed a bag, and headed out the door. She'd taken inventory looking around her room before she left. Everything she owned was gained by scamming. She felt freedom in leaving it all. Downstairs, Karen did not have the guts to come back into the room. Deep down she knew that Shardae was right. Hattie rubbed her forehead, then picked up her cell phone to call Jake. "Jake, Shardae and I just had a terrible argument and she left. She said some stuff she had in her heart a long time and I don't even want her back here. Tell your brothers to watch out for her on the streets. I got a feeling she won't be back anyway." Jake began talking a mile a minute and Hattie just cut him off, "Do what I tell you, you hear me?" Jake said, "Yes Hattie." He called his brothers with her instructions.

## Chapter #6 – "Port In The Storm"

Capri opened the door to Shardae who was bent over with a face full of tears holding a gym bag. "Can I stay with you?" Shardae asked. "Girl get in here! What happened?" Capri literally caught the weight of her body in the threshold of the door. "Daddy! Come help me!" Capri's father Daniel came rushing from his study to assist. Shardae's collapse was due to heaviness of mind, not so much the from her weight.

Daniel Brooks looked for blood, scars, and for someone who was pursuing her from behind, but saw nothing, no one. "Oh no, child! What happened? What's happening?" He asked as they ushered Shardae to a soft loveseat. He wiped her tears, but she was passed out. She came to as he was dialing 911. "Nnn...ot necessary Mr. Brooks, I'm okay. I can't live with my grandmother anymore, I just cannot!" She whispered. Capri ran to get a washcloth and patted her forehead with it wiping her tears. Daniel held her rocking her body to and fro. "It's going to be alright child. We'll talk about it. Right now, you need to catch your breath and calm yourself. Is anything hurting? Are you hurt? Somebody chasing you?"

"I'm okay." Shardae said taking slow breaths. "I'm tired of being used. I want to go to school, sir." Capri knew from recent conversations what Shardae was leading up to. She confided in Capri when she vented about her family. Capri explained, "Daddy she got her acceptance letter from Mercer. It's all she's been talking about. Shardae what happened?"

Shardae sat up straight. "It's my grandmother. She has my whole life planned cooking for her, but I want people to eat my food; my food sir, apart from Hattie!" Daniel continued to calm her then sat across from them giving his full attention. Daniel was a great single father. He supported Capri and encouraged her to stay in

school but had lost the battle when Capri's mother walked out on them both. He and Capri suffered from depression due to the messy divorce, and he was unable to convince Capri to go back. She now was slated to start Mercer County Community College having conquered the trials the divorce caused. The court awarded custody to Daniel.

Both Daniel and Capri understood the pain involved in separation from family. It had been a tough year for them. Daniel returned to work feeling a sense of renewal for them, and Capri felt she had a clean slate. She scored well on the General Equivalency. She just didn't want to repeat her senior year for her absences. It was overwhelming at the time, but they each were thriving in each other's care.

Daniel Brooks asked, "Do you want to stay with us until you clear your head? I know Hattie. I can call and talk to her if you'd like. Hattie knows who I am. She don't play with me. She didn't hurt you, did she?" Shardae appreciated the offer. She sheepishly asked, "Can I? Can I just stay for a couple of days so I can be out of that house?" Daniel told Capri to take her bag to her room so that he could talk to Shardae one-on-one.

"Shardae, the Richardsons and Brooks go back a long time. I know you don't know me well, but I knew Hattie since the 70's. We don't exactly run in the same circles, but she knows me well. I know Karen is your mom and I know all her sons too." He pointed to the front door. I hired Paul and Nathan to fix my porch steps and that door. They do good work, got a good work ethic. I don't know what Jake is doing, but Mike comes often to see Capri. He's been helping her with her the GED. That younger one seems to be alright too. Your Uncle Jake is a lot like Hattie, Karen is too. Listen, you want to tell me what happened?"

Shardae felt a lot more comfortable knowing Daniel had history of her family dating back to before she was born. There was no embarrassing secret to let out, no stigma, because if he knew that much about Hattie Richardson, then he probably knew it all. "Mr. Brooks, thank you. I was the only one who graduated in my whole family. I worked hard too. I found out I got a scholarship I ain't even apply for, my teacher submitted it. I got straight A's and one B. My uncles and my mom ain't graduate, but they were happy I did. They all work for her. My uncles have kids all over town. I am Karen's only child. I'm the only one *in* the house."

Daniel knew of the family but didn't want to make her feel bad about something she couldn't control, her family's negative status in the neighborhood. "Child, hear me well. Bad don't always come from bad. A reputation is something not easy to shake, especially here in Trenton. I know you're talented. Capri talks about you all the time. She told me you cook more than just wings. She even brought me plates of food you cooked. It made those days her momma left bearable. There's love in your food, too." He told Shardae who beamed sniffing back more tears. "I believe you have the potential to make something great happen if you were to attend college. You have a great foundation and with school you may be able to work for a good restaurant; maybe even start catering. The scholarship is a start."

Shardae had never considered what doors college would open. She just had a hunger to go. She figured she'd live with Hattie until the program was over, but she never truly thought beyond it. "Mr. Brooks?" She whispered. "Call me Mr. Dan, nobody calls me Brooks." He said. She continued, "Mr. Dan, why wouldn't my grandmother say that? Why wouldn't Karen say that to defend me when Grandma laughed about my plans? I just needed to hear that from *them*."

"No Shardae, you needed to hear that from *you*." He said standing as Capri re-entered. "C'mon Shar, let's get you cleaned up." Capri said. Daniel said, "I'm here if you need to talk. I'm going to call Hattie now. Don't be afraid, I'll just talk to her, see where her head is." Shardae managed to get to her feet and go with Capri to her room in the small 2-bedroom home. "Thank you, Mr. Dan." Capri put her arm around Shardae and they exited.

Daniel Brooks went into his study and dropped to his knees:

***"Father God in Heaven, I see my assignment clearly in this child as her mentor. Thank you for answering my prayer. More connects us than separates us. I want to do Your will, Lord Jesus. You know my heart. She's honest and caring, and I could tell that whatever happened to her today changed something inside her. Use her, Father, to bring the wisdom of You to her entire family. Use me, Jesus. I make myself available to change the wickedness of this world to Your light. Amen."***

Daniel then picked up the phone to call Hattie Richardson. "Hello, yes, Hattie...Daniel Brooks, here. Shar's here. Yes, she's here. I got her all calmed down. She'll be alright. Yes...she explained. She's going to stay a couple days until things cool, that will be best. Just letting you know she's safe. Okay then..."

Shardae thanked Capri for their kindness as Capri threw her one of her night gowns. "It's a good thing Shar, maybe it was time to leave. In the meantime, let me tackle that head, girl! You look like a scarecrow!" Shardae sat on the floor and Capri soothed her hair with a fine brush. It was so therapeutic for her. Shardae asked, "So...What's up with you and Uncle Mike???" They both laughed.

## *Chapter #7 – "Holy v Mystical"*

When morning came, Capri was up and dressed listening to music primping in the mirror. Shardae was snoring and Capri's music didn't disturb her rest. She was mentally and emotionally forfeit. Her body just shut down. Daniel had gone to work the early shift at Trenton Water Works. Capri turned with her hair held into a ponytail as Shardae stretched opening her eyes. "Good morning sunshine!" Capri greeted her cheerfully. "G'mmmg" Shardae mumbled. "Where are you going?" She asked Capri. "Nowhere." She said flopping onto the bed which made it go up and down. "What time is it?" Shardae asked. "11:15. Shardae, I let you rest because you needed it." Capri said telling her the truth.

"Yeah, I guess I did. I've got to register for my classes." Shardae said sitting up. "How long do you think your dad will let me stay?" Capri answered, "Not long. Maybe a month or so." Shardae was surprisingly upbeat hearing this. "Really? That would be generous! I'm going home, I just need a break right now. I had nowhere else to go." Shardae said. "Do you think you could find out from him for sure, because if I have to leave at the end of the week, I've gotta move quickly to prepare." Capri answered, "Well sure, I'm sure he won't mind, especially if I ask him. He knows it'll take a while to get yourself straight with classes. If he called your grandma, I know he told her in a way he won't get no kidnapping charges. You need a breather, she's gotta know that." Capri said. Shardae bit her lip, "See if I can stay, but let him know I'm not a leech, I'll pay my way. You don't think I'm a leech, do you 'Pri?" She asked with solemn eyes. "No, but you know you eventually have to go back home." Capri said standing. She walked over to her shelf which held trophies and games. She grabbed her Magic 8 Ball and shook it asking, *"Is Shardae going to ever go back home?"* They both hovered over the ball for the answer, but Capri did it for fun and was giggling. Shardae waited expectantly for the answer. The 8 Ball's dark hue revealed the message in the triangle which read, *'Not Likely'*.

Capri tossed the 8 Ball on the bed and Shardae dove for it. *"Magic 8 Ball, is Hattie going to let me go to school???"* Capri looked at Shardae strangely. Shardae's face held an intense impatience for the answer. She shook it again even harder. *"Is Grandma still angry?"*

"Shar! That was just for fun! Girl you can't take this mess seriously! I know you want answers, but you'll only know them if you call her." Capri pried the 8 Ball out of her hands and Shardae snatched it back. *"Is Grandma using me to get money???"* This time Capri allowed the floating triangle to come to the surface. *'Yes'* appeared through the window. "Shardae!" Capri swiped the Magic 8 Ball out of Shardae's hands slamming it into the wall where it rolled into the hall. Daniel, who was coming up the stairs retrieved the ball and entered Capri's room. "You girls alright?" He asked.

Shardae buried her head into her hands. Daniel put the Magic 8 Ball onto the shelf. He saw the look on his daughter's face. "What's going on?" He asked. Shardae lifted her head rubbing on the crystal charm on her necklace given to her by Hattie. Capri stood silent still stunned by Shardae's desperate need for Hattie's approval. "Dad..." She said tilting her head toward Shardae rubbing the charm. He knew what she wanted to say without words. "Shar, what's that you have there?" She looked up wiping her eyes. "It's my magic crystal. My grandmother gave it to me. It represents purity. I get healed from it."

Capri sat at her dressing table with the chair facing out. She said, "Shar, you believe in this stuff, like, for real?" Daniel quelled Capri's questioning on the subject with one look. "Oh I do! I *know* they heal, I've seen it. My grandma uses them all the time around the house. This is white crystal with rose quartz!" Shardae said lifting it higher to a place of honor showing Capri's dad.

Daniel shook his head but caught himself from being critical. "Shar, I know you were taught that certain stones have spiritual meaning and power. You've been taught about astrological signs, the stars, the moon, and the rain. Listen to me now, I don't expect you to change what you were taught overnight. I have no expectations at all. I just need you to understand that there are many things in life that are mysteries, including that crystal you're rubbing. I, myself, don't understand the metaphysical properties of gems. I understand that all the things God made with His hand are for us to use. The power of God is the only power we believe in this house."

"So I have to leave?" Shar asked. "No, Shardae, you don't have to leave. You need to know Capri and I only pray to one God, the God I Am, the Holy One. He sent Jesus to die on the Cross for our sin. He went to hell and rose again. I know that's confusing for you. Worshipping anything other than God is considered witchcraft. Did anybody ever explain this to you?" He asked quietly.

"Mr. Dan you mean like witches and brooms?" She giggled, I'm not a witch!" She said with a grin. "We don't go out on Halloween scaring people." Daniel Brooks explained with an open heart asking the Holy Spirit to guide his words carefully. "I do not believe you are a witch. I believe you have been exposed to what I see as some aspect of the *occult*, which can be dark and dangerous."

Shardae had heard the word before, but her mind conjured images of pentagrams and bat's heads being cut off and thrown into a cauldron. She was taught that crystals brought light. "Mr. Dan, this crystal is special to me, it's kind of a light for me in dark times. Whenever I rub it, it brings me so much good luck. It's not *a cult*. My grandma studies all this stuff. She can tell your future just by looking at your hand." Shardae answered smiling so proudly.

"Baby this charm has no more power than that 8 Ball up there. Nothing you can hold in your hand does. I'm not saying you're in a cult, the word I'm using is the *occult*. Dark, demonic, mystic magic. It's not of God Shardae, it's of the devil, all of it. Listen, I have to go back to work, I just came to check on you two. We'll discuss it more when I come home, okay? Here's some change for you two. Go have lunch and see a movie or something." He took Capri to the side in the hall, "My cell phone is on, and Capri, talk to her, no judging." He said leaving.

Daniel had no idea how confused the child was until she said what she said about light. He knew Hattie ran numbers, ran a crap house, ran half the city's illegal activity, but he didn't know she was a soothsayer. On his drive back to Water Works, he prayed:

***"God You must really love me to have given such a tough assignment, but I trust You will be with me. She's so young Lord, so young, but is it already too late?"*** He sat quietly as if he was awaiting an answer. ***"Nothing is too hard***

*for you, God, nothing. You were with me through so much already with Capri. I'm praying for young Shardae, in Jesus' mighty name! I know it's going to be an uphill battle. You're so worthy, Lord. I asked you to make me a willing vessel and You did. Here am I, send me. Hallelujah!"*

Shardae and Capri got dressed and went to have lunch at Ila Mae on Market Street. They ordered fried shrimp baskets and sat talking while it cooked. "Shar, I could see us running a cute li'l place like this, one day, clean food, good atmosphere, safe spot. It's hard work though." Capri said. "Yeah, me too. Only I would have the menu a little different, tables too, you got to make people want to come, you know? It's got to be inviting from the outside, some pomp and circumstance, some fanfare." Shardae agreed. "Yeah, you have such an eye for it, Shar. I could see it." Shardae got up to collect the order handing Capri her basket. She took some fries as she sat pouring tons of ketchup into her basket for dipping. "It's impossible! I wish!" Shardae laughed. "Not it's not, Sis with God, anything is possible." Capri bowed her head for grace.

"Why you ain't ask your dad about me staying?" Shardae asked after Capri lifted her head from the blessing. "Well, you were like, there. I have to ask him when we're alone. If you're there, he'll only say yes, and it may make him uncomfortable in front of you." Capri answered. Shardae slid the breading off the shrimp. "I thought that was the point, so he'd say yes." Capri wanted to get an idea of where Shardae's head was. "Earlier you were asking my Magic 8 Ball if Hattie'll let you come back home, now you're wanting me to ask my father? Girl, what exactly do you want to do?"

"I don't know, I just wish I would have shut my mouth yesterday when I argued with her. I want to go home to tell her I'm sorry, but I want to be away for a while too. I know I can't stay the whole time I'm in school, but like you said, if he'd agree to a month it would be enough. She really wouldn't expect it. As a matter of fact, my grandma is only getting welfare because she claimed me. She won't be able to do that if I ain't there and she know it." Shardae said.

"Wait, Shardae she's getting Social Services checks because you're in her household? You have no idea how much power you have right now. I thought Ms. Hattie got like pension, Social Security or something." Capri said. "Nah! She gets food stamps and a check every month, besides the money from the crap house. She reads peoples' palms, and Karen helps her with the rent. She's about to get one of the low rent apartments now though, she'll be alright without it." Shardae told Capri.

"Shardae, is that what you meant by using you? She would not be eligible for *any* of that if she doesn't have you as a dependent, and she knows it!" Capri said. "Why should you feel bad?" Shardae said, "I know, but I don't want to do her like that, though." Capri paused in deep thought about Shardae's situation. "Sis, it's just you and Karen who actually live in her house, right?" Capri asked Shardae. "Yes, but Karen gets rental assistance, so grandma just has her name on the lease wherever she lives." Capri remembered what her father said about not judging and said nothing further. "You should call her." Capri suggested. "Yeah, I think so too." Shardae agreed.

"Ma, it's me", Shardae said when Hattie Richardson picked up the phone. "Yes, Shar. I'm sorry I hit you. I just never heard you talk like that, child." Hattie said softly. "I guess you want to come home, huh? Brooks told me you were over there with Capri. Let me think about it." Shardae was not expecting Hattie to say that, especially after she apologized first. "Oh! Well I understand, Ma, I just don't know how long I can stay there." Shardae said. Hattie paused. "Well, it depends on what you plan to do with your financial aid, of course." Hattie said, "I need that to keep afloat." Shardae felt uncomfortable.

"Ma, I'm going to go to school with my financial aid funding. I thought you understood that part. You can still get food stamps and stuff as long as I'm in school." Shardae said boldly defending her stance, but Hattie asked, "What'chu wanna go to school for? You ain't better than nobody! Don't go thinking you better than somebody!" Shardae was hard pressed to understand the basis of this insinuation. "Ma, I don't think I'm better than anybody, I just want to go. It's not like with some kids who go far away for college, I'll be still living right here, ain't no campus to move to." Shardae said. She was still even tempered, talking softly as if to persuade Hattie to see it from other angles which may be advantageous, but Hattie was not interested in hearing her. "You won't be living *here*, so you better make a decision!" Hattie told her in no uncertain terms. Then Shardae lost her temper, "I don't understand! What do you lose by me going to college, Ma?" She blatantly asked, but Hattie hung up the phone.

Although Capri only heard a one-sided conversation, she knew how it went down from exposure to Hattie Richardson. Capri knew that Hattie always had ulterior motives. Shardae said, "Hello? Ma! She hung up! I can't stand her sometimes! Why she don't want me to go to school? Dang!" Shardae wiped her cheek with a napkin. "Maybe she's jealous, Shar, you said none of her kids made it out of high school." Capri suggested. "Maybe." Shardae said. "Will you talk to your dad now? It's clear I can't go home unless I work for her and not go to school. Who wouldn't want their grandchild to go to college?"

"I'll talk to him tonight." Capri said.

## Chapter #8 – "Ain't No Sunshine"

Jake and Mike set up the shed for the Friday night gambling after hour. For weeks, Friday after Friday, there was much less patronage of the spot because of Shardae's and Capri's absence. Mike set up chairs at each card table quad and Jake loaded the CD changer. "It ain't the same, man. We're taking a loss because the girls ain't here no more." Mike said. "Maybe Shardae, but Capri don't do much 'round here, she don't half be here anyway." Jake replied but Mike rebutted, "Jake, she only missed one Friday since she started, and people like to see pretty faces when they eat. They kept our customers happy, great food, that smile. This ain't even a happy atmosphere no more." Mike said. Jake said, "We gonna be alright. This Hattie's joint! People will always come to Hattie's to try to make a dollar. It don't matter, the food ain't matter; her smile ain't gonna make or break Hattie's. People want to drink and make some money." Jake said with an attitude. He retrieved the scattered balls from the pool table and racked them in the triangle. "C'mon, let me beat your butt like I used to back in the day!" Mike took off his shirt donning jeans and an A-Shirt flexing as he walked over literally thumbing his nose, "You ain't never beat me fairly, man. You always get mad and we fight. All you do is talk junk through the whole game and keep offering higher stakes. Not this time! I'm going to beat you one time, and I ain't goin' no further with it. We got enough goin' on 'round here." Mike said swinging the pool cue around the back of his neck.

"Come on! Stop bowing out before we even start! What's the bet?" Jake asked staying fully clothed. Mike said, "Alright punk! 3 games, tie breaker, loser cooks tonight! Bet?" Mike had been frying the chicken, making the sides, serving the food, and watching the door every Friday night since the ladies stayed away. "Alright! Fair enough. Break." Jake said pulling his goatee. After the break, Mike won all three games in a row as Jake talked junk making jokes and excuses. "Alright, one last game, higher stakes!" Jake taunted. "Nah, man! Get in that kitchen! I knew you would try to get out of it." Mike said dangling a toothpick out of his mouth. "Nah, man, for real! I'm cooking tonight! I just want to see where your head at."

Mike wondered what he was up to. Jake said with a sly look. "If you win this next game, I won't tell Brooks that you're hittin' his baby girl's draws every day!" Mike suddenly jumped across the pool table with lightning swift agility putting Jake in a headlock! He punched him in his face over and over. Jake struggled to get out of the hold, but Mike's fury kept him in the bent position over the pool table. "Get off man! Get off!" Jake squealed, but Mike wouldn't release him. "What do you have against her, man! Capri ain't never did nothing to you!" Just then, as Jake was turning several shades of red, Hattie Richardson walked in with a broom handle swinging it at both her sons until they separated. "What in the hell is going on here???!!!" Hattie hollered.

"Hattie, Jake started this nonsense, talking 'bout Capri! I'm sick of his crazy behind always talking about that girl!" Mike said through clenched teeth pacing. "He's mad because he still can't beat me in pool! He's gotta cook tonight! *I'm* counting the money!" Mike's jaw was held tight. Jake struggled to catch his breath grabbing his throat. "Hattie, he's been messing around with her, that's why he's always defending her! I know for a fact she's the snitch!" The toxic atmosphere was like a poisonous gas which fell over the shed.

"Cut this mess out! Y'all acting like kids! Mike, are you messin' around with Capri? She's half your age!" Hattie asked with her chest heaving. Mike placed his hands on his hips pacing. "For a good while now Hattie. She's a good girl. She's about to turn 20 in a couple of months. Her father knows I mean her no harm. I ain't even hittin' it. We have a relationship and it's growing. I would never do anything to hurt Capri! I gotta sneak to see her, man! Y'all ran her and Shardae off!" He said raising his voice, then calmed down, "Hattie, we kept it from you because we know how y'all are! We knew y'all would try to make it something that it's not, and we ain't even like that. I love Capri!" Tyrell and Nate walked into the shed as he said this, "She loves me too!" He said tearing up. Hattie yelled, "Mike, you are too old for that girl and you know it."

"What's going on?" Tyrell asked. Hattie walked over to hug him. She needed to keep order. "My family's falling apart, that's what's going on son! Go start that chicken, Tyrell. Nate find Paul and y'all get this place ready for tonight." Hattie walked over to her older sons, "Jake, Mike, you disappoint me. With all that we've been trying to hold on to, y'all want to cut up tonight? I can't take this anymore! I don't ask much of my family! We can make some good money if y'all keep your heads on straight! Y'all bringing attention to yourselves back here arguing! Wanna get raided again? Mike, go turn that dog on music down!" We don't need Shar or Capri here to keep making money! Now get to work!" Hattie yelled swinging the broom handle over her head.

"Not this time, Hattie! Y'all can run this popsicle stand by yourselves! I'm out!" Mike yelled tossing the pool cue onto the table. Hattie hollered, "Mike!" following behind him. Jake sucked his teeth, "Man, let that fool go! I ain't going nowhere, let's get ready for tonight, Ma! That boy gonna get a rape charge behind dealing with her!"

The aroma of soul food could be smelled all the way up and down Centre Street, but only a few customers came all night. Jake, Paul, Nate,

Karen, and Tyrell sat around waiting for more people, but it was a bust. They closed shop early and turned in.

It was never quite the same at Hattie's and folks started finding other after hour establishments to go to. Karen relapsed with her drug habit and did anything she had to do to feed it. She and Jake began sniffing powder cocaine hustling their street skills to get more. The family had a history of addictive behavior as far back as Essie Richardson's time. Hattie was hitting the bottle hard trying to fill the void. Hardly anyone came to her for readings after displays of drunken behavior coupled with the rumor that she kicked Shardae out of her home. She couldn't be trusted. Everybody knew she was still receiving welfare for her, so reports were being made to have Hattie investigated for welfare fraud. She was asking her children to back her lies, but none could witness for her. Nate and Paul were conveniently unavailable, Karen and Jake weren't capable, Mike refused. She seemed to have lost all credibility in Trenton. Tyrell got his own place with his girlfriend Amber who was pregnant. Paul and Nate's refurbishing offers extended to work demands in Philly, so they were barely around anymore.

Winter was approaching with no word from Mike or Shardae, and Hattie was desperate to earn cash. She tried to obtain Monica's help, but Karen was busted on camera entering unlocked cars in a State parking lot structure and had to return to County. All Hattie had left at home was Jake, who was skimming heavily off the top of any scam she had going on. As a last resort, Hattie threw her cards on the table by burning down the shed for the insurance proceeds. She was paid only $2,000. She also talked Jake's kids' mother into allowing their children to live with her, of course they became dependents for collecting welfare funds and stamps just as she did with Shardae. Their mother was an addict.

Meanwhile, Shardae thrived in the care of the Brooks family. Both Capri and Shardae attended Mercer County Community College. It wasn't easy, but they helped one another through the tough classes. Daniel worked every day at Trenton Water Works and took care of both girls' needs while they took their courses. Shardae started a job at Cheesecake Factory and was able to contribute and buy a used car. Daniel said she could stay as long as she paid her way. Both girls were due to turn a year older in December.

Daniel discussed the Bible often with Shardae who gained a natural curiosity in the ways of the Lord. She attended church with them, home Bible study, she even started to take communion. She asked so many questions about Jesus which Daniel and Capri patiently answered. They learned a great deal about Hattie's lifestyle from Shardae, like her Tarot card readings, her scams, and her shady practices such as insurance fraud. Shardae was finally able to take off her crystal charm necklace and Daniel replaced it with a Cross. She now knew the difference. On the week before Thanksgiving, she gave her life to Christ, was water baptized, and received the Holy Spirit. Many demons were expelled from Shardae who knew the enemy's only task was to steal her possibilities, kill her opportunities, and destroy her potential to become a witness for Christ.

## *Chapter #9 – "Drunken Desperation"*

Hattie Richardson banged on the door of the Brooks' home on Livingston Avenue at 11pm on Thanksgiving evening. Daniel opened the door to see Hattie's angry countenance who was standing with Jake's sad-faced unkempt children. "WHERE'S SHARDAE???" She hollered loud enough for neighbors to peek through blinds. "She's coming home with me now!" Daniel Brooks could smell the alcohol emanating from her breath. "Hattie, have you been drinking? Shardae is in the bed! Why do you have these children out this time of night?" He asked.

"Dan don't give me that bull! SHARDAE! SHARDAE!" Hattie yelled trying to get pass Daniel in the doorway threshold. "Get out of my way before I call the police!" She threatened through slurred speech. "Hattie go home! Shardae ain't going with you, and these kids don't need to be with you either!" Daniel yelled back. "Go Home!"

The Brooks' neighborhood, Mill Hill, was well patrolled. One of their neighbors had seen enough and called the police. It didn't take long for them to ride quickly down the one-way street with flashing lights. Shardae and Capri rushed downstairs and stood midway on the staircase watching Hattie try to muscle her way past Daniel to get in. Shardae yelled "Ma! What are you doing?" Seeing her grandmother in a drunken state alarmed her. Hattie squeezed the arms of the two children, who were under 5-years old, and used their bodies to thrust forward into Daniel. The little boys started crying. Shardae yelled, "Why are you pushing Jake's kids? You're so embarrassing! Stop! You'll hurt them! Why you ain't just call? It's Thanksgiving! This is their home! Stop! Please!"

Daniel stopped fighting so Hattie wouldn't hurt the children. He let them pass far enough for Shardae to be heard. "Ma! I'm not going with you! I don't care if you call the police. You look crazy right now!" Capri stood shaking her head. She said, "Ms. Hattie please take those kids home. They gonna have you locked up! My neighbors don't play!" Daniel looked up at Shardae. "Shar, you don't have to go with her if you don't want to!" The kids were bellowing loudly over their voices. Daniel held the screen door open behind Hattie, "I already see the cops coming." Daniel hollered. Two uniformed officers were walking up to the porch from a wagon with their walkie talkies blaring.

"Yes officer, this woman banged on my door disturbing us and used these children to force her way in! I want her off my property." Daniel said. "This is your property? Sir, are these your kids? Do you know this woman?" One officer asked. "Yes, this is my house, but not my children. This woman is drunk! Her granddaughter lives here. Shardae, come tell them." Shardae walked forward. The cop asked, "How old are you?" Shardae said, "I'm 17, sir. I live here with him and his daughter, Capri. That's my grandma."

The other officer took Hattie to talk to her on the porch and the children followed. Immediately he noticed that she was inebriated, and he smelled alcohol. He saw the young boys in a state of distress and took his handcuffs out of the small of his back. "These kids are with you, ma'am?" He asked. "All of them comin' home with me! I have CUSTODY!" Hattie yelled digging in her purse for official court papers, which were tea stained, but stamped with a gold seal. He said, "Hands behind your back please ma'am."

Shardae and Capri stood with Daniel Brooks. Shardae told the officer interrogating her, "I live here, but my grandma wants me to go with her. She brought my cousins here using them as battering rams to get in! She's drunk sir!" The officer depressed the button on his walkie talkie which lay upon his shoulder. He said one word, "Domestic."

His attention then went back to Shardae, "You're 17?" then to Daniel, "Those aren't your children, sir?" Shardae answered, "No, they're her other grandchildren, my uncle's kids. She just has them with her." Daniel explained that the children weren't related to him. He said Shardae was estranged from her grandmother and had been living there with them for 5 months. When he heard Hattie slur the word, *custody*, he asked Daniel, "Sir, is this a court-ordered arrangement?"

Daniel took a deep breath. "That woman banged on my door and used their li'l bodies to enter my house! But...no, sir, there's no court agreement. Shardae filed for emancipation because of ongoing issues like this. She's just a student trying to finish college. I told her she could stay here to be safe." The officer looked out and saw Hattie drunk fanning the papers with cuffed hands, He said to Daniel, "Sir, I agree that she's drunk, and she may have disturbed your home, but if she's 17, and you have no custody papers, I'm afraid she has to await Child Services with the others." Shardae's eyes widened, "Child Services? Sir, I have a job, and classes...my birthday's the 4th of December!" Capri looked concerned and couldn't remain quiet. "Sir, isn't there a way my dad can be granted temporary custody since she'll be 18 in a week and a half? I mean, C'mon! Look at Hattie! She's barely standing! All Shardae's stuff is here, she's working, she's got classes right there at Mercer!"

The officer looked around the Brooks' home seeing it was clean and in order. "It's not for me to decide...I can't. I'm sorry." He said. "Shardae, you'll have to go with them when they get here." The cop requested that the Child Services representative come to retrieve the children. Shardae flopped down on the couch crying with Capri comforting her. Daniel looked out of the screen door as a woman with a sharp suit ascended the steps. Hattie was taken to the wagon arrested for Public Intoxication, Child Neglect, and Forcible Entry. The children were placed in the woman's car by the officer. The woman talked with the boys in the car, then to the officer who stayed with the boys.

When she finally came to the door, she introduced herself to Daniel first then addressed Shardae. "I'm Barbara Fisher, Shardae. You'll have to gather some things and come with me, dear." She said.

"This is stupid!" Shardae said, "I ain't no child no more." Barbara Fisher said, "According to the State you are, but don't worry, you'll probably be right back here in a couple of days. We must let the judge decide, okay?" Shardae slowly stood, "Where am I going right now?" She asked. "You'll just be with me." Barbara told her placing her hand on Shardae's shoulder to comfort her.

Shardae hugged Daniel, then Capri. "Thank you for all you've done for me." She said, then went upstairs to collect a bag. She grabbed her phone and called her Uncle Mike who came over right away. He saw his mother in the wagon, shook his head, and entered the house. "What happened?" Mike asked Daniel Brooks, who told him the entire story. Mike had been there earlier eating Thanksgiving dinner with them as an invited guest. Capri walked over to her father and her man. Shardae came down the stairs with her bag. She hugged her uncle. They all bowed their heads and prayed together.

Barbara Fisher gave them a chance to say their goodbyes. She walked back to her car where the young boys sat with the other officer. Mike walked Shardae out of the house looking at his mother. He was her favorite. He could do nothing but shake his head. Shardae said a silent prayer for her, and they walked to the car hugging each other. All the neighbors stood around watching the car pull off. Daniel and Capri stood on the porch and Mike ran up to them. "I know this is a familiar scene, sir, Capri told me this is exactly how it was when her mother left. I'm so sorry." He said. "Shardae's going to be alright." They watched as the paddy wagon holding Hattie ranting leave.

Daniel shook Mike's hand. "Nobody's going to get any sleep tonite, son. C'mon in. Capri, try to get some rest." They went into the house together and Mike and Daniel stayed up talking all night. Daniel began to learn the history of the Richardson family and everything which seemed to plague them. Mike was a great historian. He described each metaphorical tree branch of the family from Essie on down to Shardae. He spoke of how his family had never done business legitimately, and how this criminal mentality just seemed to trickle down through the generations.

"How old is your mom, Mike?" Daniel asked. "She's 61. She had Jake at 13, my sister Karen at 17. Their father got swindled by Hattie a long time ago. She took that fool for everything he had, but then she met my father a decade later. I'm 29. She had Nate & Paul the next year, and Tyrell was a surprise to all of us. Grandma Essie called Hattie a gypsy because she moved from house to house so much. Grandma Essie sold tobacco cured with whiskey and got hooked on it. She dipped snuff too. I remember her walking around spitting in that tin cup. Hattie got a lot of her ways."

Daniel wanted to dig a little deeper. He knew Mike trusted him but didn't want to seem judgmental. After all, it was his family, and we can't choose to be in one. "I see. Is reading palms one of the things Hattie got from Essie?" He asked. Mike felt comfortable revealing all.

"Before I met you," Mike said, "I was used to seeing all of that thinking it was normal. Hattie was always superstitious; not just the normal avoiding the number 13, walking under a ladder, stuff. She wouldn't do anything on the 13th at all. She put stock in her lucky number, too, 4, mostly, because she was 44 when Shardae was born on the 4th. She's her only granddaughter. She had one daughter out of all of us rockhead boys. Essie only had one, and Karen was the only one of us who had a daughter too. She kept that baby covered in crystal! She even asked Karen to name her Crystal."

"So…Mike, before me, was there anybody who talked to y'all about God? I mean, did y'all ever go to church?" Daniel asked with his hand on Mike's forearm. Mike shook his head, "Nah, never. Hattie wanted us to get paid. She ain't care about no church. We grew up with a rabbit's foot tied to our shoelace. God wasn't in our house. Dan, I didn't go to church until you took me. There's not a Bible, no Cross, no Gospel music nowhere in Hattie's house. You come home with friends, they see Tarot cards and crystals, plumes of black feathers, dream catchers, and devil's horn, that's it. Hattie's got stuff Essie brought over on the stagecoach. I remember she took us to what I thought was a church when we were small, me, Karen and Jake. The entire altar was made out of bundled twigs. The man came out all in black and put a glass of water on the altar. We stared at that glass for 2 hours!"

Daniel was listening intently as Mike continued. "We went to what Hattie called 'camp.' Everybody was naked, and an old couple got branded with a pentagram on their butt cheek. Everybody celebrated! It was crazy. We don't...talk about this stuff. It's just not talked about, but I remember all of it. I remember snakes in baskets. I even remember Essie carrying snakes around her wrists! She took us to a compound where we all learned to shoot. Essie's husband taught us to clean guns and shoot." Daniel now understood the depth of this one family's demonic possession. "How old were you when Essie died?" Mike answered, "I was 6. She died in jail."

Daniel placed his large hands on the dining room table to stand. He asked Mike, "Son, do you want to be free from all that confuses you about that mystical life? Free from the guilt and shame of it, free from the torment, forever? Jesus can turn it all around right now." Mike stood sobbing as if he was a 6-year old again. "I do sir, I admit, I was only going to the church to see Capri, I'm so in love with her. I never expected to learn so much about God! I never had the opportunity to! I don't want to feel like this anymore!" Mike cried out falling onto Daniel hugging him like he was his father, then Daniel stood him up straight up by holding his shoulders like a man looking into his eyes.

He walked over to his China cabinet taking out his Holy anointing oil. He placed his hand on Mike's head, thanking God. "Raise your hands, Mike. Surrender." He said softly thanking God. He asked him, "Do you believe what you heard in church? That Jesus gave His life on the Cross for your forgiveness? That He rose after He died to give you everlasting life? Do you believe He's alive now after conquering the grave?" Mike collapsed in his arms, "I do! I receive Him, sir!" Mike cried pouring out years of pain and heartache onto Daniel's shoulder. "I believe it!" Daniel saw that he was sincere fully embracing him. It was deliverance for him, and he felt he could actually hear the angels around him. Daniel prayed a powerful prayer over Mike in the name of Jesus.

*"Father God, in Jesus' mighty name, search this boy's heart and mind. He desires to be free from the enemy's curse forever! Remove anything that is not like You, Father God! In Your Word You said demons tremble at the name of Jesus! You have given us the authority in Jesus' name to rebuke demonic spirits attacking us! This long-lived curse who has wreaked generational havoc on his soul has to leave! I command you demon! In the name of Jesus! Leave him NOW! You will no longer possess him, his household, his children, his niece, his mother, brothers, or sister! In the name of Jesus! My God you are stronger than any curse placed on his family! I cast you out! Right now! Jesus Your shed Blood conquered hell and the grave on the Cross! You are Way, the Truth, and the Life! Hallelujah! You took every sin, every curse, so he can be free and live! You said, 'It is finished!' I believe You! He accepted You as His personal Savior! Father, thank You! The heavy chain of this generational curse ends this day with Him! Don't let him be the same! This, I pray in Jesus' name! Amen."*

# *Chapter #10 – "Discovery"*

Shardae woke up knowing she was in a strange place. She had been dreaming about Hattie. Her little cousins were on a roll-away bed, head-to-foot across from the bed she awoke in. She searched her cell phone for missed calls and messages seeing a one from Capri asking if she was okay. Despite the hour she texted back, 'I'm okay. I'm at that lady's house, not a facility. Keep you posted.'

She kneeled at the foot of the bed praying. Shardae thanked God first, then asked the Lord to look out for her grandmother. She prayed for her mother and her uncles. She prayed for the two sleeping not far from where she knelt. For herself, she told the Lord she trusted Him. She was finished her prayers, but something strange popped into her head, 'Prudence'. It was then that she remembered the Tarot cards she had drawn from her grandmother's deck.

"Get behind me Satan!" She said aloud. She physically shook it off. ***"God, I know you created me uniquely, I accept that. I know I am not Essie, Hattie, or Karen. I am Yours, Father. I know that you removed all that from me as far as the east is from the west. Your plan for me is unique. I just want my family to be okay. I just want to be okay. I trust You for my life, not those mystic demonic cards. Amen."***

She sat listening for the Holy Spirit to guide her as she often did. Shardae had come to trust Him. She said to herself, 'Wait! Who am I hearing from? Those voices that tried to kill me?' then began to pray aloud, ***"Jesus You gave me authority! I shall not be moved! I stand on what You promised, Lord! I shall NOT be moved! I am the head, and not the tail! I see your ploy, enemy! Get behind me! You can whisper that old life to me all you want! I*** *shall not be moved! I'm the righteousness of God! He stripped you of your power against me! I have the victory! Praise Jesus! The God who levels strongholds made me the curse breaker!"*

She heard her phone vibrating and knew that it was a reply from Capri Brooks. 'Call me asap!' Shardae walked around with the phone peeking in the hallway to find a spot where she could have privacy and not wake up the boys. Barbara Fisher was in the hallway. "Good morning Shardae, are you hungry?" She asked. "What time is it?" Shardae asked. "Your phone's in your hand, dear, it's 7am. I have to get you guys ready to go." Shardae's hand began to itch and she scratched it from her palm all the way up her arm. "Where are we going?" She asked Barbara.

Barbara reluctantly said, "To a state-run facility where you will be housed until court. I'm sorry, it's just red tape. This was a one-night deal." Shardae said, "This is stupid. By the time there's a court hearing, I'll be an adult." She turned away to get her cousins up and washed.

When Shardae had herself and the boys ready, she explained to them that they'd all have to go to a special place with Barbara Fisher. She told them the place would have lots of toys and kids to play with. They were excited about it. They all ate oatmeal and headed to the facility in Barbara's car. It wasn't far, and the boys were surprised to see that they had been there before. Shardae hadn't. She hugged them when they were separated from her running to a familiar colorful room with a large busy beads table.

"Shardae, we're in here, this is the office where they will discuss what will happen. Be patient. She's a good person. I have to pull a couple of files for research. I'll return soon." Barbara Fisher said asking her to sit by the office door in a long corridor. "Yes ma'am." Shardae said.

A woman opened the door after all of 3 minutes and asked her to come in. She closed the door behind her. "Hello Shardae, I'm Rasheeda Stokes, come in, have a seat." Shardae sat. "I understand you attend Mercer for Culinary Studies, is that right?" Rasheeda asked. "Yes, ma'am." Shardae answered. "It's my first year. I'm missing class right now!" Rasheeda Stokes looked at her. "You'll be 18 on the 4th. I consider you a special case. It's clear you have the capacity to handle yourself as an adult, according to Ms. Fisher. You're in school, you have income, no children of your own; I talked to the Family Court judge in mediation overnight. It's both Mrs. Fisher's and my recommendation that you see the judge today. You're hearing starts in an hour." Rasheeda said. Shardae was trying to keep up with her words carefully. "Today?" She asked.

Rasheeda continued without answering, "Shardae, I will be advocating for you as your court liaison so we can get you set up in your apartment while you work and complete Mercer. You're in a certification program, correct?" She asked, but Shardae was numb and speechless hearing those words and couldn't answer. "For the first year, your rent, bills, food, and other accommodations will be paid for by Social Services. We will monitor your progress during that span of time, though you will be an adult. Do you disagree with anything I've said, do you understand?"

Shardae's eyes were as big as quarters. She asked, "You mean, I'll…have my own place? Like my own?" She smiled with excitement. Rasheeda said, "Well, yes. Social Services will foot the bill for any expenses you may have for a year from December 4th 2019 to December 4th 2020. Do you agree with our decision?" Shardae smiled harder, then heard the Holy Spirit speaking. "Ma'am, when you say Social Services, do you mean like welfare?" She asked. "Well, yes. Right now, you're considered a ward of the State until we see the judge, who will emancipate you as an adult. You are eligible to receive help until you can live independently." Rasheeda informed her.

Shardae knew immediately that if Hattie came over to the Brooks' home a week later, she would have already been considered an adult and would have struggled a long time. She thanked God for the opportunity, but she felt extremely uncomfortable receiving welfare. Shardae articulately expressed gratitude but felt conflicted on *how* Rasheeda wanted to help. "Ma'am I agree to see the judge so that I can be officially removed from my grandmother's custody. I also appreciate you setting this up so I can be on my own, but I don't really want to be on welfare. Mr. Brooks told me that it's a trap that Black people fall into and never get out of. My great-grandmother, my grandmother, and my mother, they all were on welfare! I don't want to be on welfare all my life. As far as rental assistance, I can pay my own way."

"Shardae dear, please understand", Rasheeda explained, "You are an employed person who needs help. Everybody needs help from time to time. This is not a handout or lifestyle we're offering. This is an agency giving a child with no competent parents a fresh start. By you working, you have contributed to the workforce, which means you are a taxpayer. If today was December 4th, I would not be able to help you at all, understand?"

Shardae had never considered herself a taxpayer. She worked only to help her grandmother and got paid cash under the table. Even throwing Mr. Brooks a couple of dollars to stay under his roof she never really realized she contributed to the workforce. She felt she was paying her way. "Yes ma'am. I do. I want to finish my Culinary program and still work though, is that okay?" She asked. Rasheeda smiled, "That's more than most people who sit across from me want. We'll wait for Ms. Fisher to return and then go to the courthouse. Do you need anything right now?" She asked. Shardae was filled with emotion and could not accurately form words. She breathed in the word 'taxpayer.'

Just then, Ms. Fisher came in with a look on her face that would wake Essie Richardson out her grave! "Shardae, would you please excuse me and Ms. Stokes for a minute?" Barbara Fisher asked Shardae, who got up and sat in the hallway again. She was excited and complied with her request out of respect. The woman had let them stay in her house and fed her well. Shardae was grateful for Thanksgiving irony.

When the door was closed, Barbara Fisher presented Rasheeda with several reports detailing the criminal legacy of Hattie Richardson and her direct connection to Shardae. "You're not going to believe this!" Barbara Fisher exclaimed. Rasheeda sat reading page after page of how Hattie had lied to authorities such as Social Services, Social Security, and the Family Court about Shardae's birth and education. She had faked doctors' signatures on reports stating Shardae was born with significant brain disabilities and was incapacitated needing specialized long-term care. To each entity, Hattie had reported ongoing progressive health issues Shardae was supposedly suffering each year with a progressive status being mentally and physically incapacitated, which was well documented from birth to present records with highlighted sections in detailed descriptions.

The birth report listed her as, 'often evaluated by medical professionals for long term care', with phrases such as, 'requiring around the clock care', and 'constant nursing supervision', and even 'child requires protective headgear and other pertinent respiratory apparatus.'

In a lawsuit filed in 2004 by Hattie Richardson against Mercer Hospital, (Capital Health), records indicate birth resulted in brain damage due to hospital negligence by the ER OB-GYN and the Maternity Ward Neo-Natal Department. Lack of prenatal care, long term drug use and neglect by the mother, Karen Richardson, who apparently abandoned the baby after birth which contributed to other significant disabilities. Hattie Richardson claimed custody and visited the hospital's Neo-Natal Ward for months until the baby was to be released to *CHOP*.

Other descriptions highlighted in reports of Ms. Fisher's research were phrases like, 'child not likely to viably thrive', and 'recommendation: admittance to institution' were discovered. The report listed the baby's physical description and defects as, 'birth weight 2.4 lbs., blood type O Neg, eye color brown, club foot, cleft lip & palate, missing fingers, deafness, blindness, birthmarks, skin café au lait, and respiratory issues', along with other descriptions which clearly do not match Shardae's as this thriving 17 year old who Ms. Fisher had seen for the past 15 hours!

The reason Hattie had been adamant about Shardae not pursuing higher education was that the lawsuit would be thrown out, ineligible, null and void, and frivolous if she had gone to college!

Rasheeda said, "This child would never have been able to achieve this status with these health impediments listed." It was easy to conceal in her mainstream records for public school by falsifying documents. Hattie was to receive an undisclosed settlement on the child's 18th birthday. "She's been receiving disability for this child since she brought her home from the hospital!"

Coincidentally, it was discovered that an African American female born at home in a neighboring town delivered by a doula had gone missing the same day this baby was discharged into Hattie Richardson's care. The parents were from Sierra Leone. The 8-month old baby was taken in the middle of the night causing a 17-year nightmare for the young couple. Rasheeda couldn't believe what she was reading. In a matter of hours, Barbara Fisher had discovered the abscence of one baby and the kidnapping of Shardae!

Barbara Fisher whispered, "Hattie Richardson is not aware that we know about these records. If someone would have taken the time to review them, it would have been discovered much sooner!" In addition to her other charges, a concealed weapon in Hattie's bosom was found by the female officer when she was hauled in.

"How do we…? Barbara Fisher tried to ask a plethora of questions at once, but Rasheeda looked at her watch and yelled. "Let's go! Court is starting. Judge Moss is waiting!"

## *Chapter #11 – "I Am With You"*

Before Rasheeda and Barbara came out of the office, Shardae finally had an opportunity to return Capri's call. "'Pri? What's going on?" Capri screamed into the phone! "Girl! Your grandma on the front page of the Trentonian! Tyrell called me telling me to tell you not to be alarmed, he thought you were still here!" Shardae said, "The front page??? I got missed calls from Tyrell, I couldn't answer! I'm about to go to court!"

Capri said, "Amber is in labor right now, too, he had to go, he told me and went back into Labor and Delivery! I ran out and got a paper, my dad's at work! Shardae, you okay? You're at court?" Shardae could barely get a word in, but she stilled her emotions and maintained her composure. "Capri, what does the paper say?" "It's says 'FRAUD' in large letters across the front with a picture of Hattie from like 10 years ago looking like she on her way to church! On the side, there's a picture of your cousin Cecil Clark and a picture of some White lady, Judith Pig-a-something! Piga-Piga…" Shardae knew that her cousin and Monica Frein had also been arrested in connection to Hattie. She said, "Pigliano", Capri said, "Yes!"

The newspaper article described Hattie as not only a greedy opportunist who preyed on the system for welfare fraud, but a professional scam artist taking advantage of low-income housing opportunities who had gotten away with her crimes for three decades! Where the article continues in the center of the paper, there was the list of pending charges including conspiracy, money laundering, insurance fraud, forgery, jury tampering, securities fraud, and weapons charges as well.

Shardae said, "Yeah, she's the front for Ma's business, Judith is her fake name, her real name's Monica. She gets money for her, I guess they don't know her real name yet. Cecil pretends to hire employees at Amazon and gives Karen work ID's. So, Tyrell's girl in labor? Wow! Karen ain't in the paper?" Shardae asked. "Nope!" Capri answered. Shardae said, "She will be. Monica will snitch on her to make her charges go away. I tell you girl, I feel bad, but I feel good, too. These people talking about getting me my own place! They're going to pay my bills for a whole year, too. I'm sad about my grandma, I mean, the whole Trenton knew anyway! She's been in that paper so many times, but she's probably going for good this time. It's like getting the worse news and the best news on the same day! They're going to help me, *and* I get to stay in my classes and keep my job! Uncle Jake's going crazy I know it!"

Capri said, "Yup somewhere talking junk! Tyrell couldn't tell me where nobody was! I asked about Paul and Nate, he said they've been in Philly. Mike's been here with us since last night. Daddy said Mike starts working with him next week. Shardae he got saved!" "Capri, I got to go, they're coming out to take me to court now." Shardae said. Capri said, "Okay, keep me posted so I know what to tell my dad!"

Shardae was overjoyed by the news her uncle received Christ and got a job with Daniel, but she had to put that and the Trentonian aside to prepare her mind for the hearing. She wouldn't have to say anything because the Child Services reps would speak on her behalf. Barbara Fisher had a Trentonian tucked under her arm as they walked to the elevator. As the elevator descended, Shardae was able to scan the newspaper article with one glance, though it was folded upside down.

Before the elevator doors opened, Shardae asked, "Can I see your paper?" Barbara handed her the newspaper engrossed in conversation with Rasheeda. Shardae cleared her throat, "Excuse me." She said begging their pardon holding up the paper for them to see. "I don't think I can go through with this." She said solemnly. The ladies stopped talking and looked over at her. Rasheeda rubbed her back and gave her an encouraging look. Barbara looked as if she would cry for her after learning Hattie was her kidnapper. In that moment when the elevator was still, the Holy Spirit spoke to Shardae's heart,

**'I am with you.'**

It was five to eleven, and they were all walking quickly to get to the courthouse a block away. They made it to Judge Moss' courtroom but Shardae was told she'd have to sit on one of the outer benches and wait. The ladies rushed in as the bailiff said, "All Rise...Judge Jack Moss presiding." The heavy court doors closed and Shardae looked around at the empty corridor. Nobody else had court this day, the day after

Thanksgiving. There was only one clerk behind the glass partition farther down the end of one hall. "How did they do this overnight?" She asked out loud. "This was You, Jesus. Your hands are all over this. Thank You!"

She sat and read the entire article of Hattie's shame. Shardae had seen everything that was written in real life up close, and there was so much more she knew about which could have made this 3-page article a hundred-page New York Times best seller. She filled in the blanks in her mind of what wasn't reported. Shardae told God, *'I hope I'm never called to testify for or against her.'*

45 minutes after the doors closed, they opened. Rasheeda Stokes came out smiling and Barbara Fisher held Shardae's hand. "The judge would like to meet you, Shardae. He thinks you're a remarkable young woman. In my experience, judges don't see children. You're an emancipated minor now, well, at least until your birthday! Barbara said with a humble smile. They both held her hands walking into the empty courtroom. Shardae's heart pounded.

"Shardae Richardson?" Judge Moss addressed her. "I remember you. I presided over Hattie Richardson's last case before I was transferred here to Family Court. Do you understand what Child Services has asked of me today? Was everything explained to you?" He asked.

"Yes, your honor, I do. I don't take it lightly. Yes, they explained, sir." Shardae answered. "I remember you, too." The judge continued, "This is a new beginning for you. I'm sure you've seen the morning newspaper. Think of today as the end of one life and the beginning of a new one. I'm not just being loquacious. You literally have a fresh start young lady." Shardae held her head up with pride. "Thank you, your honor." She said. "The stipulation is that for the span of a year, despite you being an adult, Child Services will monitor your progress in college and at your employment, at your state-run apartment, and in your social life. Do you understand?" Judge Moss asked.

"Yes, sir, I agree, and thank you!" Shardae said. "Shardae, there's going to be some tough days which you will face, and soon. Child Services is going to take you for a medical examination, bloodwork, and to the apartment campus. Do you have any special requests?" He asked. Shardae thought of asking, 'Could you make sure I don't have to testify against my grandma', but she knew better. "Sir, I just want to thank you, Ms. Barbara, and Ms. Rasheeda for helping me. I wish I could cook all of you lunch one day." Shardae said smiling. "I wish you the best of luck, dear." Judge Moss said sounding sincere but had a look of deep concern. He banged the gavel and it was over.

The ladies took Shardae to lunch at Olive Garden, then to the medical facility, and finally to the apartment campus. They each extended an invitation back to Olive Garden for her birthday to celebrate and she happily accepted, "I'd love to!" She said looking forward to it. They took her to her 2$^{nd}$ floor apartment unit which was supplied with basic essentials from dishes to bedsheets and allowed her to shop at a local dollar store for any personal needs. She was taken to the Brooks' home to get what was left there. They were both so happy for Shardae.

The following day, The Trentonian's front page held mugshots of Karen and Jake Richardson in connection with Hattie's crimes. The paper described Jake as a confidential informant which the police often paid for information, including the reports supplied by Jake before the Lamberton Street raid of Hattie's. Shardae was not surprised. She knew he blamed Capri for snitching when it was him all along. He wanted Hattie out of the way. Shardae's four remaining uncles helped her move into her place along with Daniel and Capri Brooks. She was proud to cook for all of them to thank them.

On December 4, 2019, Rasheeda and Barbara came to take Shardae to lunch. After they ordered, they carefully broke down what they thought she could handle, that Hattie falsified records when she was about eight months old, born of a Sierra Leonian couple, which was confirmed by blood typing and DNA. Shardae was told that who she thought was her family was not related to her at all. They told her that it was Jake Richardson who had kidnapped her at Hattie's request after he had stalked African-born women who chose not to use hospitals for the birthing process. Seven couples were stalked. Hattie settled on the course with the least obstacles to steal Shardae from their Greenwood Avenue home.

Karen's baby was smothered to death not even a week after being released from CHOP into Hattie's custody. Instead, she chose to do what she always chooses; to enhance her criminal empire for financial gain by using Shardae as a new stream of income throughout her life. Shardae was told that the corpse of Karen's baby was found buried on Federal Street. More charges were added to Hattie, Jake, and Karen.

Shardae felt her entire foundation had been rocked. She appreciated the ladies, but to learn of this on her 18th birthday sent her into a tailspin. She lamented over Karen's baby and Hattie's incarceration and she didn't speak much during the rest of dinner. Rasheeda tried to comfort her by expressing optimism. She asked Shardae to look at the bright side, that she had a real family to explore who had a deep desire to speak with her to build a relationship. Shardae said she needed time. Barbara Fisher volunteered to mediate for her birth parents and for Shardae. She knew they had her best interest, but it was something like being hit with a sledgehammer, and she just requested time to absorb the shocking information.

"Day by day, I've been getting impactful, life-altering news about my own existence. I will have to continue to trust the Lord. I appreciate you ladies taking me out today, and it does feel like a fresh start. It's nice to receive mail in my own mailbox. I feel pride when I clean my home, lock my own door, even taking the trash to the dumpster. It's my trash. I love my grandmother, even though she used me. I still love my uncles and Karen who I thought brought me into the world. I am not ready to meet my birth parents yet. I just need time, if that's okay." Shardae said.

Shardae's birthday was bittersweet. For a week, she tried to study undistracted. She had a gourmet cuisine final coming up soon which needed her focus. She also had what she felt were the oddest work shifts at the Cheesecake Factory. Her car badly needed service. She hadn't visited to see Tyrell and Amber's baby. It was all overwhelming. She needed to keep going but felt like she had a target on her back. It seemed since she'd heard the news that she was a kidnap victim, she couldn't quite adjust to the many obstacles which seem to be coming her way. Her patience with Capri, peers at school, and coworkers was short, out of character for her. Shardae had realized that she was wearing herself thin but could not drop work or school to maintain compliance with the court agreement.

She talked to Daniel Brooks about what was going on. He was the one person who she could answer truthfully when asked, 'Are you alright?' She told him all she had been dealing with and the news of her birth, the murder, the kidnapping, and feeling guilty, in addition to this overwhelming feeling of heaviness. Daniel told her the truth. "Shardae, it's when you begin to serve the Lord that the enemy will dispatch more powerful agents to deter your progress.

The closer to your goals you get, the more obstacles will arise. What you have to do is take all you're feeling, bag it up, and place it down at the Altar. Give it to him! He wants you to have abundant life. If we were to handle all our problems, we'd end up in an insane asylum. That's not what He intended when you gave your life to Christ. Expect that the closer you get, the more the devil will try to separate you from Him. Praise helps, genuine praise. Keep your eye on Him, he'll handle everything else." Daniel knew what she had meant by heaviness. He decided it was time to address it with Capri, Mike, and Shardae at one time.

Shardae woke up in praise and worship taking Daniel's advice. Suddenly, she found herself putting on the full armor of God before even leaving for the day. She anointed her home with sweet smells and bought artwork depicting Scripture for her walls. Her apartment differed vastly from the home she was raised in. She never missed an opportunity to thank Him for turning her life around.

She started to feel the protection of the Father, Son, and Holy Ghost surround her, and it was like the lumps in her oatmeal began to smooth out nicely before her. She knew she was enjoying a closer Christian walk in maturity. She talked to God in her apartment like she'd talk to Capri, speaking plainly about His plans for her life. She said, ***"Father, it's like we were all on this endless carousel ride, and I just wanted to get off. Nobody ever got off! Essie must've learned it all from her mother, and it just went around and around, right on down to me. I don't want my children to ever get on this carousel!"***

Shardae called Mike who she knew heard the news about the baby switch. "Uncle Mike?" Shardae said, "I know you heard, but I still love you and you will always be my uncle, no matter what." Mike didn't say much, as usual. He loved Shardae and it didn't matter to him either, he replied, "I love you, baby girl. There's nothing that will ever change that."

## Chapter #12 – "The Sweetest Card Ever Dealt"

Daniel, Capri, Mike, and Shardae held Bible study at her new apartment campus. Shardae made up a flyer and posted it in the common room on each floor of the building inviting residents to join. No one came, but they all agreed it wouldn't be the last time it was posted.

Shardae grilled salmon, asparagus, and made cous cous. They had peach cobbler for dessert. Daniel decided to delve into Ephesians which he felt was needed observing the melancholy atmosphere. He had started with Ephesians although they had been studying Corinthians for a month. Daniel began the Bible study with prayer thanking God for fellowship among them, then began to read Scripture.

**Ephesians 4:32~ "Be kind and compassionate to one another, forgiving each other, just as in Christ, God forgave you."**

To have started so subtly and quietly, the participants thought it would be an easy session. Corinthians was a breeze! It was easy to understand and apply in everyday situations. They all shifted in their seats uncomfortably when the Ephesians Scripture was read.

Daniel asked, "Mike, who do you feel you need to forgive?" Mike answered, "I need to forgive me. As you all know, I spent time in jail when I was young and hardheaded. I'd put a gun to anyone's head for Hattie. I just...I just need to forgive me. I'm not who I was."

"Shardae?" Daniel asked. Shardae said, "Mr. Dan, that's not fair. I'm not ready. I'm still feeling numb, do Capri." She rocked back and forth in the folding chair and sipped lukewarm tea. Daniel said, "Turn in your Bibles to **Mark 11:25**. Capri read, please." Capri read the Scripture boldly, **"...And when ye stand praying, forgive, if ye have ought against any: that your Father**

**also which is in Heaven may forgive you your transgressions."**

"Shardae, In Matthew, how many times did Christ say we should forgive?" Daniel asked. Shardae thumbed through Matthew having memorized the Old Testament and New Testament Bible order. "Um...which Chapter, Mr. Dan?" He quoted the Scripture having learned it by heart since he was a child, ***"...And Jesus answered, I tell you, not seven times, but seventy times seven."***

Everyone realized what Daniel was doing. They had all been hurt in various ways by people who they loved. Capri immediately understood she needed to forgive her mother for hurting her and her father, Mike could only picture Jake's face at that moment, and Shardae began to cry out and it echoed off the common room walls. "I know I was forgiven for so much!!! It's so hard, Mr. Dan, so hard! Why did she use me??? She hurt me so much! I just don't want to see her anymore, but I still want her to be alright! It doesn't make any sense! Jesus forgives me so easy, and it's not fair!" She bellowed out all her feelings and Capri hugged her so tight. "Dad", Capri said, "I forgave her a long time ago, I just don't want to ever see her again. I forgave her for me." Concerning her mother. Shardae said, "She killed that baby and stole me! How am I supposed to forgive that?"

Daniel smiled at Capri and looked to Shardae. "You feel the weights drop off of you when you forgive others." Shardae knew exactly what he meant. "I forgive her, Mr. Dan, I just want to love her from over here. I hope she does understand what she robbed those people of, what she robbed me of; but I do forgive her. I…guess I can now leave my tithe at the Altar. I got to talk to her, huh?" They all giggled at Shardae, but it let Daniel know Shardae was studying her Bible on her own. That had not been covered in their studies. They embraced one another and the trio left Shardae's apartment full of the Spirit and full of her delicious food.

When everyone was gone Shardae sought guidance from the Holy Spirit about meeting her birth parents for the first time. She had seen them in the newspaper but avoided reading the article. They were also on the local news channels. For the first time, she wanted to know more about them and their homeland. She decided to contact Barbara Fisher to request a meeting.

At the meeting held at their home on Greenwood where she was abducted from,

Shardae, accompanied by Barbara Fisher sat with Dinni and Maggie Selasie, but it was certainly not their last visit together. The Selasies were overjoyed in finally meeting Shardae sharing birth photos and Christening announcements. They were so heartbroken over their missing baby and no clues were ever found which lead to Jake or Hattie. They were eternally grateful to Ms. Fisher. Shardae watched as her birth mother's hand movements and expressions were like her own. Her birth father was an excellent cook and made sure everyone knew it was he who had prepared the hors d'oeuvres. She was sure that these fine people would never, ever hurt her after that first visit. They just wanted to be a part of her adult life.

She learned she has an older sister, Siambe Selasie, who lives with her husband in California and works as a Master Chef at a fine restaurant. Shardae was excited to see photos of Siambe which looked so much like herself. She thanked God for her birth family.

Shardae had finally completed her Culinary Studies certificate program May of 2020 with a Grade Point Average of 3.81. She wasn't able to celebrate with the Brooks family or the Selasie family due to quarantine restrictions due to

Coronavirus, which spread quickly to all corners of the earth. The virus shut down public gatherings. Everyone had to adhere to social distancing restrictions and wear masks to quell the contagious spread. Many were vulnerable to the virus and deaths rose daily during this terrible pandemic. Coronavirus, or COVID-19, is a respiratory disease which altered the lifestyles of every human being on the planet. Testing for the virus was in high demand for those who exhibited symptoms, but researched vaccines were hard to acquire and very expensive.

Wearing facial masks and handwashing was promoted as a preventive, but most medical professionals explained that no one is immune and eventually everyone will experience it. It was paramount that those who were vulnerable carefully limit their exposure to even family members. Seniors, those with compromised immune systems, and residents of facilities like penal institutions were especially vulnerable.

Shardae was saddened to hear that before she had an opportunity to visit Hattie Richardson, she died of the virus just before Shardae graduated from Mercer County Community College. Shardae was not able to attend her funeral or comfort her uncles for quarantine restrictions. She grieved alone but felt horrible that she was not able to tell her she was forgiven before she died. It wasn't for lack of effort, Shardae was never placed on her visitor's list. Hattie was serving two life sentences for her crimes having escaped the death penalty by one juror's vote.

Every year on her birthday, Shardae received cards, bouquets, and cookbook recipes from Barbara Fisher and Rasheeda Stokes. Shardae was forever welcome at the Selasie home receiving invitations each holiday until the Coronavirus stayed her.

When she sat alone in her home one day, she wrote a series of figures on an index card alpha-numeric to see if her memory had weakened. She left the card on her counter face-down and watched a TBN program. She returned to the counter and flipped the card glancing at it once. She took out another index card and wrote what she thought she saw. She had every digit correct. "I still got it!" She yelled tearing up the cards. Hattie Richardson popped into her head while she was still giggling. 'Lord, I sincerely hope someone in that prison taught Hattie about You, I really do. If she had only used those same skills legitimately in the corporate world, she'd probably be another Madam C J Walker!' she said scratching her palm.

Shardae thought about what she had just thought about Hattie, and the Holy Spirit told her to apply the logic to herself. There was this big wide world ahead of her with few obstacles. She had broken the curse of the carousel ride by finishing school, maintaining employment, maintaining her own residence, was a bonified taxpayer, and she had so much support from Capri, Daniel, Mike, Paul, Nathan, Tyrell, The Selasies, Barbara and Rasheeda.

God had given her special gifts, talents, and desires. Opportunities were presented with Him in control for her life, an abundant life! Shardae dropped to her knees, ***"Father God, I have the desire to open my own restaurant. Systemic oppression is no excuse to live a slothful life! I have no desire to scam anybody and I can easily avoid being scammed because of what I've been through. If you think I can do it, so do I!"*** Shardae raised her hands in praise. ***"If it be your will, Lord, help me to learn what I need to do to accomplish this. I'm standing on Your promise! I thank you Jesus! Amen."*** As usual, Shardae waited for the Holy Spirit to answer praising God for what

was ahead. She claimed her successful restaurant in authority in Jesus' mighty name!

That winter, Paul and Nathan visited Shardae about her request to find a place where she could establish a restaurant venue. She was told about a small property which they were renovating in Bromley at the old site of Club 10, which was closed down for many years. They had bought it, but did not know exactly what they intended when they bid on it months prior. They told Shardae they knew where they could *legally* acquire most of the equipment needed to open her restaurant at the Pittman Avenue site. They said they'd help finance anything they could not obtain. Tyrell would even help run the restaurant with her. He was still a new husband and father, but it would be advantageous for them both. Mike would be able to safely secure it in the evenings.

Shardae was ecstatic! She began shouting praises to God for opening so many doors for her; the opportunity to further her education, her cooking skills, her connection to the Richardson, Brooks, and Selasie families, all of it contributed to who she was. The twins didn't understand the praise, but they were happy that she was happy. Shardae recognized the opportunity to tell them about how God worked in her life from the time she accepted Jesus. They both were excited for her but couldn't understand.

Nate said, "Shardae, baby girl you turned yourself into one of those God-happy fanatics, huh? You're just as bad as Mike!" He and Paul exchanged looks laughing. Shardae said, "Absolutely Unc! When you've been delivered from what *we* were exposed to, you can do nothing but be a God-happy fanatic!" They still didn't understand her. "You both are witnesses to what my God can do. He uses vessels like you to get His work done in me because I believe. I believe!" Paul said, "...As bad as Mike? She's worse than Mike! That fool threw out all Hattie's crystals and Tarot cards!"

Shardae said, "Jesus Is The Sweetest Card Ever Dealt!!!!! Get to know him for yourselves."

# Carousel

*Trisha E Williams*
*IreeSky Fiction, LLC*
*IreeSky.com*